Billionaire Unmasked

THE BILLIONAIRE'S OBSESSION
Jason

J. S. SCOTT

Billionaire Unmasked

Editing by Faith Williams – Atwater Group
Cover by Cali MacKay – Covers by Cali

ISBN: 978-1-939962-50-8 (Print)
ISBN: 978-1-939962-49-2 (E-Book)

Contents

One Night With a Billionaire

Chapter 1 1
Chapter 2 17
Chapter 3 25

Billionaire Unmasked

Chapter 1 39
Chapter 2 51
Chapter 3 64
Chapter 4 77
Chapter 5 89
Chapter 6 102
Chapter 7 115
Chapter 8 124
Chapter 9 134

Chapter 10 141
Chapter 11 151
Chapter 12 158
Chapter 13 168
Chapter 14. 176
Chapter 15 185
Epilogue 193

One Night With a Billionaire

BILLIONAIRE UNMASKED
The Prequel

J. S. SCOTT

Chapter 1

Midnight, New Year's Eve, Amesport, Maine, 2014

Hope Sinclair desperately tried to draw her eyes away from the most attractive man she'd ever seen, and failed miserably. She knew him, had known him for most of her childhood, but she wasn't a child anymore, and *sweet Jesus!*—neither was he.

Dammit. I have to stop staring at him. I'll look in another direction in just a minute. I will. I will stop drooling over him.

Still, her eyes stayed riveted on Jason Sutherland, unable to pull her gaze away from the most breathtaking man on the planet. Hope tried to be subtle by taking a sip of champagne while she stared, but she was fairly certain her lust was pretty obvious. He was enthralling when he sported a pair of ripped jeans and t-shirt. In a tux at a New Year's Eve party, he was overwhelmingly beautiful, heart-stopping—in a very male, unconsciously seductive kind of way. It wasn't just his gorgeous face and ripped body that made women stare; it was the entire package. Every action, every word that came out of his mouth exuded confidence, a bold masculinity that no woman could seem to resist. His expression was predatory and cautious as he conversed with another man at the party, no sign of the sweet, genuine smile she knew he was capable of flashing. Obviously, he wasn't talking to someone he knew; it was probably someone who wanted something from him, like most people generally did.

Her breath caught as she watched him nod his head abruptly at the man and stroll over to her brother, Dante. His expression morphed, changed into the charming man that she knew Jason could be. He slapped Dante on the back and gave her brother a genuine smile; his eyes warmed as he appeared to joke around with Dante.

The many faces of Jason Sutherland.

She sighed, and finally ripped her gaze away from Jason, wondering how many people actually knew the man beneath the billionaire exterior. Hope hadn't seen Jason often in the last several years, but he couldn't have changed that much.

Hope had decided long ago that she adored Jason. She had wanted to marry him at the tender age of seven, and her feelings hadn't changed much over the last nineteen years—except for maybe the wanting to get married part. Oh yeah, and the lust part which had popped up suddenly when she'd seen him at eighteen. Now, at the age of twenty-six, she *still* thought he was the most devastatingly handsome, dangerous man she'd ever seen.

Granted, Jason wasn't slaying her dragons for her anymore. He wasn't stopping the bullies who'd picked on her in grade school because her hair was just a little too red, her freckles a little too noticeable, and she was just a little too awkward to fit into the popular crowd of kids at school. Back then, Jason had been larger than life to her: her older, wiser twelve-year-old superhero who came to her rescue any time she needed him. And one of the things she had adored most about Jason? He had *never, ever* told her older brothers about *any* of those humiliating experiences. The guy could definitely keep a secret. As close as he'd been to her brothers back then, Jason never divulged any information to Grady, Dante, Jared, or Evan if she'd asked him not to tell. If Jason *had* let her brothers know what had happened at the snobby, private grade school she'd been forced to attend at the time, her brothers would have gotten involved, and they would have ended up in trouble. Adding more strife to her brothers' lives back then would have just given her alcoholic, abusive father more reason to create chaos—not that her constantly angry parent had ever really needed a reason. Still, Hope hadn't wanted to rock a boat that was already sinking. Life in the Sinclair household had been plenty miserable without adding any of her childhood problems to the drama.

Then, when she'd turned twelve, everything had changed. Jason had gone off to college later that year, and she'd been devastated. But like any twelve-year-old girl, she'd eventually gotten over the loss of her idol, seeing Jason only during his brief visits back to Boston. During her teen years, he'd become more of a friend or acquaintance who she saw occasionally, someone who existed only on the fringes of her teenage years. At least…he had, until she'd seen him again at her high school graduation, a day when all thoughts about her childhood icon and casual friend shifted and completely altered the way she felt about Jason forever. He wasn't a god or a buddy anymore after that day. Nope…her hero-worship had turned into something far more dangerous when Hope had turned eighteen:

Lust!

Mortified at her body's reaction to seeing him, she'd managed to hide her attraction to him over the years. It hadn't been that difficult. She rarely saw him, and usually avoided any event that she thought he might attend. She wasn't always successful, and there were some meetings she couldn't avoid, but she'd always had a boyfriend, and showing her carnal thoughts about Jason had been an impossibility.

He lived in New York, and although she traveled for her crazy lifestyle, New York City was never one of her destinations, so casual encounters didn't happen because of geography. It was a long way from her home in Colorado to New York City. More often than not, she ended up in the middle of nowhere to pursue her career, definitely not places where Jason would be on business.

Hope was yanked from her thoughts as the volume of the party grew to a roar.

Five!
Four!
Three!
Two!
One!

The clock struck twelve and the large hall exploded with noise.
Happy New Year!

Hope smiled as she lifted the glass of champagne to her mouth and took a long, slow sip. Grady, her brother, gave his bride-to-be, Emily, one of the most passionate kisses Hope had ever witnessed.

I'm glad I came. It's so nice to see Grady so happy.

Hope had hesitated over leaving Colorado and coming to Amesport for Grady's engagement and New Year's Eve party, even though she owned a second, larger home here. It was a busy time of year for her, she was in a bad state of mind, and all Grady had to do was mention that Jason might be coming, and she'd balked. However, she'd wanted to see all of her brothers, and Grady had been the first brother to fall in love and get engaged. Now, she was grateful she'd taken the time off to come to Amesport. Her brothers were more important than some ridiculously embarrassing attraction she had for Jason. It wasn't as if she and Jason were enemies. In fact, they were virtually strangers now, though they'd once been friends.

At important times like these, no matter how busy the Sinclair siblings might be, they were all united. Hope had needed to be here. She hated how separated she felt from her siblings because of the way she lived her life; that yawning distance hurt. Being able to witness Grady's happiness was worth every uncomfortable moment of being in the same room as Jason.

Seeing Grady like this is so worth it.

Grady's new fiancée was lovely, and Hope flushed with embarrassment as she thought about the problems she'd caused between the newly engaged couple. Her brother Jared was a manwhore sometimes and sent unwanted females in Grady's direction. Hope had rescued Grady several times by calling his house and pretending to be his wife; she'd been bitchy enough to scare every one of them away.

❦ ❦ ❦

Unfortunately, when Emily had answered Grady's phone, Hope had mistakenly assumed that Jared had sent another woman in poor Grady's direction, and she'd played the same part. Problem was, Grady had wanted Emily. *Oops!* Luckily, Emily had forgiven her, but Hope was still mortified.

One by one, her brothers came over and bussed her on the cheek, and she hugged every one of them tightly while she returned their embraces. Even though they all drove her completely insane with their highhanded older brother attitudes, she loved Evan, Grady, Dante, and Jared with every fiber of her being. If only they weren't such royal pains in the asses sometimes. Being the only female in the Sinclair family, and the youngest, Hope was completely screwed when it came to protective older brothers. They had constantly bitched about her now ex-boyfriend, James, because he didn't have a job. To them, anyone less than a successful, wealthy man who worked like a fiend, was a loser unworthy of her.

They'd forget all about James if they knew what else I was doing. I'd get more than constant lectures.

Her heart ached that she couldn't and wouldn't share much of her life with her protective older brothers. It had put a certain distance between them that she'd never wanted, but had created by not sharing much of her life with any of them. It wasn't that she didn't want to. She ached to really have them be part of her life. But the price of telling them everything would be way too high.

Hope sighed and took a long swig of her champagne as she thought about her lonely existence. Somehow, her life had turned out way different than she'd imagined when she graduated from high school and had finally gotten free of the home that had been a prison to her.

If I'd only known back then how things would turn out, I might have done things differently.

Now, she wasn't a prisoner of her critical mother anymore; she was held captive by her own deceit.

Merriment was rampant all around her, everyone ringing in a brand new year. She had a jovial smile on her face, but Hope had never felt more alone.

"Thank God Hope finally dumped the loser boyfriend." Dante needed to yell to be heard over the loud roar of the partygoers as they celebrated New Year's.

Jason Sutherland's head jerked up. His body tensed. "Hope broke up with her boyfriend?"

Dante nodded. "Right before she left Colorado. Asshole. Who breaks up with a woman at the holidays?"

Jason's fists clenched in reaction. "Did he dump her?"

Dante shrugged. "She didn't say much. I don't think she wants to talk about it. I'm just glad he's finally out of her life."

Dante's attention was taken by his brothers, and Jason turned his back on them. His eyes sought and fought Hope as she stood alone by the bar and sipped a glass of champagne.

Jesus, she's beautiful.

His chest ached, which wasn't unusual when he saw Hope. It had been that way for him since the day he'd seen her at her high school graduation.

I should have stolen her away then.

Every event where he'd seen her after that day had been fucking torture, and this party was no different. He'd finally had to turn around just to keep himself from going to her, stripping her naked and making her his right here and now.

Hope Sinclair was his private obsession, a woman who could change him from a rational thinker to a possessive, compulsive maniac with just one look. She wasn't *trying* to be provocative. She didn't need to. Hope *was* provocation personified to *him*, just by standing where he could see her.

And for the first time since he'd seen her at her high school graduation, she was available.

Fuck. That made her totally irresistible.

Jason's heart squeezed as he watched her: smiling, yet solitary, just like him. He wondered whether she felt as alone, restless, and edgy as he felt right now.

His eyes roamed over her, from her swept-up auburn hair, to her generously curved body, and finally to those sexy stiletto heels that made him have delusions of fucking her as those heels dug into his ass, her calling out his name as she tipped over the edge of a powerful climax.

Shit! I can't do this anymore.

His fully erect dick jerked with impatience and pushed powerfully at the zipper of his tuxedo pants. Luckily, he wore a jacket so the whole room couldn't see his secret sexual fixation on a woman who should be taboo for him.

She's Grady's little sister.

Jason had been friends with the Sinclairs for as long as he could remember; he'd grown up close to them in a very exclusive neighborhood in Boston. Grady and Dante were very good friends of his, but that alone hadn't kept his dick in his pants when it came to Hope, although it *had* been a deterrent. The biggest obstacle had always been her boyfriend. Jason didn't share, and if he had Hope Sinclair, he'd never be able to tolerate thoughts of another man in her head while he was fucking her. Besides, he knew Hope well enough to know that she wasn't going to screw him while she was still involved with another guy. Jason had suffered in silence, his deep-seated need for her kept in check—just barely—every time they met.

She's available. No more boyfriend.

He almost literally felt the stopper on his desire pop free, leaving his body burning to bury himself inside Hope and claim her like a rabid caveman. His eyes narrowed as he watched her intently. It was beyond time for him to make his move.

Mine.

Determinedly, he set his drink on a table and made his way over to Hope, single-mindedly driven to claim her before he completely lost his mind.

"Happy New Year, Hope." The velvety, rich baritone was so close that Hope could feel the hair at her temple flutter as heated breath hit her cheek. Her body shuddered with an involuntary response as large, warm hands landed on her shoulders firmly and turned her around to face the voice.

Yes, she'd watched Jason all evening, her eyes glued to his tall, muscular body, immaculately dressed in a black tuxedo that he wore as casually as he would a pair of jeans. But being this close to him was unnerving for her. Jason Sutherland was more than comfortable in his own skin, no matter what he wore. It was something that had always attracted her to him at any age. However, up close and personal, and with Hope way beyond the age of hero-worship, he made her pretty damn edgy.

He was too perceptive, too discerning, and his penetrating azure eyes always seemed to be able to look clear down to her soul. It was uncomfortable for her and made her uneasy around him for most of her adult life.

"Happy New Year, Jason," she murmured and smiled at him politely.

Oh God, he smells good.

Hope felt the heat pulsating between her thighs just from inhaling his musky, woodsy scent, the essence of male pheromones that could make a woman drunk just from breathing him in. It was all she could do not to close her eyes and let herself drown in his *fuck-me-now,* deep voice and masculine smell.

She tilted her head back, and she was captivated by his liquid blue eyes. The color reminded her of the sky on a perfect summer day. At a fairly average height of five foot five, and adding on another three inches for the torturous heels she wore, Jason still towered over her and made her feel overwhelmed when he was this close to her. Defensively, she took a step back; his hands fell off her shoulders.

Jason registered a quick look of disappointment before it was gone, replaced by a mischievous grin, a smile that nearly melted Hope's panties from her body.

"I want my New Year's kiss," he said, his voice nonchalant, though his eyes smoldered.

No. Not happening, big guy. If I get that close to you again, I'll get lost in your scent, drown in those baby blues.

Hope knew if she let him too close to her, the carefully built façade that she'd worked so hard to perfect over the years would crumble. But she knew she couldn't refuse completely. She had no reason not to kiss him. He was, after all, a family friend. Carefully, she took a tiny step forward and presented her cheek to him.

Jason closed the distance between them and took her champagne glass from her hand. He set it on a nearby table. "That's not exactly what I had in mind, beautiful." Taking her hand, he didn't say another word as he led her to the balcony doors on the other side of the room, and spirited her outside.

Perplexed, Hope halted as he closed the door. They were alone on the patio. And it was damn cold out here! She was dressed in a fairly conservative black cocktail dress with long sleeves, but the hem flirted with her knees, and the cold air rushed up her skirt to chill her entire body. She rubbed her arms and shivered. She was rapidly turning into a block of ice. "What are you doing? Are you crazy? It's freezing out here." She ground her teeth from the cold.

Immediately, he divested himself of his tuxedo jacket and wrapped it around her upper body, using the lapels to draw her closer. "I needed privacy, and I'll be more than happy to warm you up," he answered, his voice husky and mysteriously urgent.

Hope luxuriated in the jacket, still warm from his body heat.

Dammit, it smells like him.

"Why did we need to be out here?" she asked, confused. "You could have just—"

He brought her whole body, jacket and all, against his warm, solid form, and cut off any protests she was going to make when his mouth covered hers. Hope's toes curled in her painful, three-inch heels as Jason took possession of her lips and speared a hand into her shoulder-length auburn hair. The clips that had held it off her shoulders flew into the air as he devoured her. She gasped in surprise, which gave Jason the opportunity to deepen the kiss, tilt her head and explore the recesses of her mouth with his tongue so thoroughly that it took her breath away. Her damn treacherous body took over and responded as if her life depended on it; her arms wrapped around Jason's neck and she surrendered to his embrace. He commanded, and she complied, letting him ravage every one of her senses as she responded to his dominant exploration, and reveled in it.

This is what she'd wanted, what she'd needed from Jason since her high school graduation, the day she'd finally admitted to herself that she was hot for him. He'd never made a move on her, never treated her as anything other than a friend, but she'd wanted...*this*. She'd felt the sexual tension between them since the day she'd seen him at her high school graduation party. Not sure if the longing was just coming from her or both of them, she'd avoided any kind of close contact or intimate conversation with him ever since she realized she wanted him. Now, she knew the attraction was mutual. The proof was hard and firm against her lower abdomen. She wasn't sure whether she wanted to celebrate or run for the hills. The sensations she experienced from his carnal embrace were new to her, as exhilarating as they were frightening.

In the end, Hope's traitorous body made the decision all by itself. Her female hormones did a victory cheer as she let her fingers slide into the coarse texture of his hair and yanked his mouth harder against her own.

Closer. I need to be closer to him. I need this. I need him.

She let her tongue duel with his, gave herself up to the moment. Jason was taboo, her secret fantasy come to life, and she let herself wallow in the passion of the desperate touch of his lips as he conquered her mouth. He brought her body to life for the first time in a very long time, and with far more intensity than she'd ever experienced. With Jason, there was no slow burn from his passionate kiss; she felt incinerated, overpowered by his masculinity, the heat between them completely consuming.

Finally, he pulled his mouth from hers. Both of them panted from the out-of-control encounter.

"That's why I needed privacy," he told her hungrily. His face was buried in her hair and she quivered from the heat of his breath on her neck. "Watching you from across the room was killing me."

Coming back to reality, Hope tried to pull away from him. "Jason, I—"

"Don't," he growled. His arms tightened around her. "Don't tell me that you didn't want that and a whole lot more as much as I do."

She couldn't tell him that, because it would have been a lie. There had been enough lies in her life. She hadn't expected her body to respond to desire like this, but she had a volatile reaction to Jason. "I did want it. If I didn't, you'd be screaming in pain right now from me nailing you in the balls with my knee."

And God help me, I do want more. But I can't. I can't do this.

She would never give herself over completely to physical desire, and she knew instinctively that with Jason, it would most likely be all or nothing. He was never tepid in anything he did, and she was fairly certain he'd want everything from her.

A low husky chuckle vibrated against her ear. "I'm happy to know you haven't changed much," he said, amused.

Oh yeah, I have—you'd be surprised how different I am. "You don't know me anymore." She pulled back slowly, to wean herself off the incredible feel of his body against hers.

He grasped her by the shoulders, and wrapped her more tightly in his jacket. "Maybe I don't," he conceded. "But I want to catch up. I want you. Spend time with me tonight, Hope. Let's go on an adventure together like we did when we were kids."

That comment hit like a bolt of lightning to her heart. Her little adventures with Jason had been the highlights of her childhood. Granted, most of their so-called adventures ended up in the local candy store because Jason was addicted to chocolate, or the ice cream shop because she'd begged him to take her, but Jason had always made those simple excursions seem like crazy expeditions. Looking back, he'd been a very good sport about playing a sea captain or an explorer when he was already in high school, just for her amusement. "I'm not ten years old anymore," she muttered unhappily.

"Believe me, I'm well aware of that fact," Jason replied darkly, enigmatically.

Hope put her hands on his muscular biceps. She looked up at him and searched his expression, able to decipher very little in the dim lights of the patio, except for the hint of desire that lingered in his eyes. "Why? You have women falling at your feet on a daily basis. Why me? Why now? You could pick the most gorgeous woman in the room back there if you want to kill some time." Jason Sutherland was a billionaire investor, and at the age of thirty-one, he was one of the most sought-after bachelors in the world. Even if she *was* an old family friend, why did he want to spend any time with *her*? Although Hope owned a home here in Amesport, Maine, she didn't live here, and Jason had flown in just to attend Grady's engagement and New Year's party. Both of them would leave in the morning. Maybe he was just restless and bored. Still, there were plenty of attractive women inside for him to pick from if he just wanted a one-nighter. She couldn't give him what he wanted, and she wanted more from him than she was capable of accepting. Jason made her crave him like a highly addictive drug, but she knew she was unable to absorb him like she wanted to do.

Jason shrugged. "I did pick the most attractive woman at the party, and I don't need to kill time. I just don't feel like pretending tonight, Hope."

The profound sense of loneliness in his voice echoed in her soul. Hope wasn't even going to act as if she didn't know what he meant. She knew. Jason was surrounded by people, lived in the world of the mega rich, but Hope knew from experience that it was difficult to know what people's motives were when they claimed to be a friend, or when they claimed to care. Most of the world they'd both grown up in was superficial at best, which was why she avoided the media and chose to live outside of that sphere as an adult. However, Jason didn't have a choice. He was a little young to retire, and it wasn't part of his personality anyway. He was driven, and always had been.

Hope lifted her hand to his face and stroked over his rugged jawline. She loved the feel of the stubble beneath her fingers. "You have more to offer than money," she told him softly, honestly. Beneath his brutal, businesslike exterior, Jason had the heart of a man who had done just about anything to cheer up a grade school geek who had been bullied during her childhood years. He'd even been willing to make a fool of himself when he was supposed to be a cool high school kid. That heart still beat in this man's chest. He'd just learned to cover it well with social ennui and the "kill or be killed" survival instinct in business, just like her brothers had.

"And what else do I have to offer?" Jason asked gruffly. He wrapped one strong, muscular arm around her waist again while he traced her lips absently with his index finger.

You mean something other than the fact that you have a good heart and the body and face of a god? Um...you mean other than the fact that you're hot enough to melt almost any woman's panties right off her body? Oh yeah, and did I forget to mention that you're also freaking brilliant?

Jason wasn't just attractive; he was every woman's secret fantasy. She'd never seen him naked, but she had no doubt he was breathtaking. It wasn't difficult to see that he was ripped, even with his clothes on, and his broad shoulders and over six foot height made him appear dangerous and formidable. His golden hair was several different shades of sexy blond, and it was cut in a style that made him look constantly mussed up. It was amazing that he could make that style so damn sexy and sophisticated, even in a tux. Okay... *especially* in a tux. On Jason, the cut was polished and urbane, even if it was a "messy hair" look that made every woman— especially her—want to rip off his clothes and take him to bed just to make him look even more disheveled because he could rock that particular look so damn well.

"You have a good heart, Jason," she finally answered, distracted by the sensual feel of his finger on her lips and the look of hunger in his eyes. She thought it was best to leave out the hotness factor for now.

He threw his head back and roared with laughter.

"What? You do," Hope answered firmly, getting annoyed.

He sobered slightly and shot her a wicked smile. "I'm an asshole, Hope."

She couldn't dispute that. Anyone who was as rich as Jason had a part of them that was ruthless. "Just on the surface," she mused quietly. Her hand fell from his face and to his shoulder.

He fiddled with a lock of her hair, his expression pensive. "You'd be surprised how deeply the asshole part of me goes." He let out a masculine sigh. "My sweet Hope, rescuer of all creatures in need, do you want to try to rehabilitate me?" he asked woefully.

Jason didn't need to change. He just needed someone who understood him. She cringed at his description of her, but sometimes she *was* a sucker for any animal or human in need. Almost always, that particular characteristic actually ate at her soul because of the path she'd chosen to take with her life. "I still have Daisy," she confessed. Jason had brought her the mostly white kitten with a few tan spots when she'd seen him at her high school graduation. Daisy had been pathetic and starving, abandoned on the side of the road. Jason had brought her to Hope, and she'd never had the heart to get rid of Daisy. It had been love at first sight for her and her faithful companion.

"I thought you were going to fatten her up and find her a home," Jason remarked knowingly.

"I couldn't." Not that Hope had tried very hard to get rid of the kitten. In fact, she'd never tried at all. It had only taken her five minutes to fall in love with the adorable baby feline. "She's deaf. Nobody wanted her," she added defensively as Jason gave her a skeptical look. Her blue-eyed cat couldn't hear, but it didn't slow Daisy down. The kitten had probably been deaf since birth, and didn't seem to miss something she'd never even had. However, Hope could never let her out of the house because of the danger of the cat being outside without being able to hear any imminent danger, a fact that didn't seem to faze Daisy at all.

"I'm sorry," Jason said remorsefully. "I never meant to saddle you with a deaf cat."

"Don't," Hope said hastily. "I love her. She's good company." It wasn't easy for Hope to have an animal with her travel schedule, but she managed with the help of her next-door neighbor when she couldn't take Daisy with her.

"Better company than your ex-boyfriend?" Jason asked in a disgruntled tone.

Oh yeah…him.

"Definitely," she countered adamantly. Jason ran his finger sensually down her cheek and she shivered.

"You're cold." Jason took her frigid hand and led her to the door back to the party. "Let's get out of here. Come away with me," he said persuasively as they reached the door.

Come away with me.

I just don't feel like pretending tonight.

Hope looked up at Jason, searched his eyes, tried to figure out his urgency. His expression was cocksure, his jaw still hard-set, but there was a look of persuasion in his eyes that she couldn't ignore.

I can't. No, no, no. Not with Jason. I can't let that slightly pleading light in his eyes get to me.

In the end, it was her own heart that betrayed her. "Okay. I'll meet you out front. But I'm not sleeping with you, so if you just want to get laid, don't show up." Something troubled Jason, and she wanted to know exactly what was going on with him. Besides, she *wanted* to be with him. They were both leaving tomorrow, and it would probably be a long time before they ran into each other again. Even though being alone with him was dangerous, it was also such a compelling temptation that she couldn't resist. Beyond the lust, she'd missed *him*.

I only have tonight.

"That's not *all* I want," Jason answered ominously as he opened the door for her.

Apprehension ran down her spine like a cold finger as she noted the deep timbre of his voice and the fact that he didn't deny that he wanted to sleep with her. She handed his jacket back to him. "So you won't try to seduce me?"

"I most likely will at some point because I won't be able to stop myself, but you can always say no," he told her gravely.

That was the crux. I'll have a hell of a time saying no.

She straightened her shoulders, and gave him a disapproving look. "I have no problem saying no," she lied as she skirted the room to avoid the crowd.

"Hope?" Jason caught her arm gently from behind.

"Yes?"

"It will still be a good night, even if you do say no. I just want us to spend some time together." His voice vibrated with intensity.

Damn. Damn. Damn. I'm sunk.

He'd sealed her fate with those words. Just that statement tore through her defenses like no other words could. Jason actually wanted her company, too, and it touched her. She could sense his loneliness, and she wanted to assuage it by letting him know she just wanted to be with *him*.

Without another word, Hope turned on her heel and went to say goodbye to her four brothers and Emily before she grabbed her jacket and exited the Youth Center where the party was being held.

By the time she arrived outside, Jason already waited for her. As she took his outstretched hand and felt the *zing* of electricity spark between them, she hoped to God she wasn't going to regret this night.

Chapter 2

I'm never going to live through this night.

Jason Sutherland had to swallow a groan as he watched Hope sit in front of the fireplace in her house and moan as she took her first bite of the s'more he'd created for her. He watched her eat the graham cracker, melted chocolate, and toasted marshmallow concoction: her eyes closed, and her tongue darted out to catch the drops of chocolate and marshmallow that stuck to her lips. Never had chocolate seemed so erotic.

Fuck. I want her.

Jason's possessive instincts nailed him in the gut, and he could barely contain the gnawing desire to have her closer, lick those delectable lips himself. He'd be at the task long after the damn chocolate and marshmallow were gone.

I shouldn't have come to Maine tonight. I knew she'd probably be here.

Yep. He *had* known, and if he were honest, he'd admit that her being here was part of the allure that had brought him to Maine. Sure, he wanted to see the Sinclair brothers, especially Grady because he wanted to meet the woman who had captured his reclusive friend's heart. But he'd be lying to himself if he didn't admit that knowing Hope was going to be here was both a deterrent…and a temptation. The appeal of seeing her again had won, the victory against his willpower coming pretty damn easily.

Disgusted with himself, Jason had tried to forget the tortured lust that had hit him when he'd seen the eighteen-year-old Hope. *Christ.* She'd just graduated from high school, and although he had only been twenty-three then, it had still seemed…wrong. Hope was Grady's baby sister, and Jason was friends with the entire Sinclair clan. Hope had been a sad, shy little girl, an adorable redheaded, freckled child with a big heart who Jason had always wanted to coax into smiling. He'd adored her like the sister he'd never had, and had protected her like any big brother would. Even so, everything had changed when he'd stopped by her high school graduation party. The sight of her threw him off balance and confused their whole relationship. He'd wanted to claim her then; now, eight years later, the desire was a damn obsession. Unfortunately, his dick hadn't forgotten Hope either. He hadn't felt that kind of all-consuming carnal lust since he'd seen her at eighteen, but his cock had immediately come to attention once again with the same fervent adoration the minute he'd spotted her across the room tonight.

Over the years, he'd cringed every time he heard from Grady that Hope was seeing someone. Jealousy nearly ate him alive every time he saw her, knowing another man was touching her. But he'd coped with it by working and fucking other women; he hoped that eventually that niggling fear that she'd end up permanently taken by another man would pass.

It hadn't. His craze to possess her had just gotten stronger, deeper. And now he was in Hell.

If this mania had been for any other woman except Hope, he would have seduced the female a long time ago, tried to fuck her out of his system. Problem was, it *was* Hope, and he'd known her almost as long as he could remember. So he was utterly and irrevocably screwed at the moment. Not only did he want to fuck her worse than he wanted to breathe, but he actually *liked* her. Hope was one of the sweetest females he'd ever known, and her big heart was genuine.

She wants me, too.

Her body had responded to him, and that made him even crazier. That the sexual chemistry burned hot both ways made it almost impossible for him not to touch her.

"Thanks for taking me to the fireworks."

Hope's voice interrupted Jason's lustful thoughts. After they'd left Grady's party, they'd driven down to the beach and had watched the fireworks from his rental car. They held hands like teenagers because he couldn't seem to completely let go of her now that she was here... and unencumbered. Admittedly, Jason had watched Hope more than he'd watched the sky lighting up with brilliant color, but her face had been so expressive that he couldn't help himself. "I'm glad you enjoyed it," he finally replied huskily.

"Didn't you?" Hope asked curiously. She finished the last of her s'more and licked her fingers. "Aren't you going to make one for yourself? I know you want the chocolate. That was delicious."

Fuck! Not the finger licking. Is she trying to kill me?

As he watched that pink tongue stroke over her fingers, he wished that she'd put it to work somewhere on his body, preferably south of his navel.

Jason willed his dirty mind to shut the fuck up. It *had* been a good night and he didn't want to spoil it. What he'd told her earlier was true. With Hope, he didn't have to pretend to be someone he wasn't. They'd come back here to Hope's house on the Amesport peninsula after the fireworks, after they'd stopped by the all-night market to get the things they needed to make s'mores. They had both changed into jeans and sweatshirts before settling themselves by the fire. "I will," he agreed. "I was just busy watching you. You look like you enjoyed it." Jason had enjoyed it, too, but he now sat on an unrelenting hard-on.

"I did." She nodded her head. "I don't let myself have chocolate very often anymore."

"Why?" He shoved a marshmallow onto the toasting stick and held it over the fire. Not having chocolate every day was unfathomable to him. He craved it almost as much as sex. Well...not nearly as much as he craved sex with Hope, but badly enough to make sure his supply was always stocked.

Hope rolled her eyes at him. "I think I have plump genes. I'm not exactly thin, Jason."

Jason's eyes roamed over her body covetously. She appeared to be in good physical shape, but obviously no amount of exercise seemed to trim down her curvy hips and rounded ass. *Thank God!* Supermodel thin had never really been attractive to him, and he was glad she'd never lost the appealing softness of those hips and her ass, not to mention those plump breasts of hers. She was fucking... perfect.

"I think your genes look just fine," he answered hungrily. She was curved in the right places. Her soft, warm body fit against his as if she'd been designed to be there. "You're beautiful."

She gave him a surprised stare, and for just a moment, Jason got lost in her emerald green gaze, her eyes liquid and soft. Her fiery hair framed her beautiful face. Jason wondered whether *that* was how she'd look when she came for him.

"You're on fire," Hope exclaimed, half amused, half alarmed.

It took Jason a second to realize she meant his marshmallow. He pulled it out of the flames and blew out the fiery blob. "I like them burnt," he lied shamelessly as he smashed the blackened marshmallow between the chocolate and graham cracker. Just the melted chocolate made it worth eating the burnt marshmallow.

She wrinkled her nose at him as she watched him eat the gooey mess. "How is it that Dante hasn't come looking for you? Aren't you staying with him?"

"I never asked him. He probably assumes I'm staying with Grady. And Grady probably assumes I'm staying with Dante. I'm hoping they don't talk about it." Every one of the Sinclair siblings had a home here on the peninsula, although Grady was the only one who lived here full-time.

"You can stay here with me. It's not like I don't have the space," Hope told him earnestly.

Jason had his private jet parked at the airport outside of town, his pilot ready to leave whenever Jason was ready. "I'll probably just fly out. The jet's on standby."

"Unlike the rest of you, I had to actually fly a commercial plane like most normal people do," Hope teased. "Evan is taking me back to Colorado, though. And then he's flying on with Dante to California. He has some business there."

Jason swallowed the last of his burnt marshmallow s'more. "Why is it you never wanted me to manage your funds for you?" Hope had never asked, but he would have been happy to invest her fortune like he'd done for Grady and Dante, built her sizable inheritance into billions. It was what he did best—making *some* money into *a lot* of money.

"The money never meant that much to me, and you're busy. Money is nice when I need something, and it lets me have my freedom. But I don't really care if it grows or not. I have more than I could ever spend in a lifetime, even if I was extravagant, which I'm not."

"I'm never too busy to take care of you, Hope. What are you doing with the funds?" he asked gruffly.

She explained how she'd stored her fortune once she'd received it and Jason cringed. Not one penny was in solid stocks or investments. *Christ.* "Money market accounts and bank accounts aren't making you much money, Hope." The investor in him recoiled in horror. "I can't believe Evan didn't step in."

"Nobody needs to step in," Hope replied angrily. "It's my money and I don't care how fast it grows. I told all of my brothers that, and they finally stopped hounding me. I rarely spend any of it. The only things I've purchased since high school are a small condo in Aspen and my vehicles. I went to college, remember? I can actually work."

Shit, she looked fabulously irate. Her green eyes flashed fire at him, and it just made Jason even harder. Hope had always been independent, which was why her loser boyfriend had always been a mystery to him. She was sweet, but she'd never been the type to put up with a lot of crap from a man, even her bossy brothers. "You're not working right now. You need to be generating more income," he argued irritably. "Especially if you're going to keep picking guys who don't have a damn job." *Fuck*. That rankled. There was nothing that annoyed him more than thinking about *any* man except him touching Hope.

"I am—" Hope clamped her mouth shut and took a deep breath, not finishing her comment. "I'm doing fine," she finished more calmly. She averted her gaze away from Jason's face.

"Are you really fine, Hope?" he asked fiercely, breaching the short distance between them to grasp her chin and force her to look at him. "Or are you feeling just as damn lost as I feel right now?" Jason knew his control was slipping, but he couldn't bring himself to give a shit. Who watched out for Hope? She'd just split with her boyfriend. Was she heartbroken? Was she happy in Colorado? Why did she stay there if her relationship was finally over?

"I'm doing good," she answered quietly and looked into his eyes this time.

"What about your ex-boyfriend? How can you be okay?"

She shot him a weak smile. "I think it was time. We just weren't right for each other. I'll get over it." She paused. "What's happening with you, Jason? Is something wrong? You seem…troubled."

For some reason, the fact that Hope sounded like a concerned friend made him completely insane. "Nothing's wrong, but I definitely have a problem."

"What?" Hope asked gently.

"*You*," he growled as he grasped her hand and pressed it against his throbbing erection. "I can't stop wanting *you*. I've wanted you for what seems like forever. I can get on my goddamn jet and fly back to New York, but distance isn't going to work anymore for me. I'll be thinking about you anyway, getting myself off on fantasies of being so deep inside you that you can't think about anything else but me." He snaked his hand behind her neck and covered her mouth with his before she could say anything else, or deny the heat between them. He came completely unraveled as she straddled his lap, pushed him down to the carpet, and covered his body with hers. She fisted his hair and kissed him as if her life depended on it. Her tongue met his stroke for stroke, as if she had never felt physical desire before and had to have it—now that she'd discovered it.

He grasped her hips and pulled her heated core against his erection, cursing the denim that separated them. Her silky hair caressed his neck and fell like a curtain around them as they exchanged an embrace so desperate and needy that he groaned into her mouth.

Need. To. Be. Inside. Her. Now.

Finally, Hope tore her lips from his. "I think I have the same problem that you do," she murmured breathlessly. She buried her face in his neck and ran her tongue over any bare flesh she could find.

"Jesus," Jason rasped, stunned but euphoric that Hope was actually this raw and out of control. He kept her straddled over his lap while he sat up, grabbed the hem of her sweatshirt and pulled it over her head. With the front clasp of her bra released, he watched as her breasts sprang free: plump, ripe, and beautiful, the raspberry-colored nipples already pebbled with desire. "Beautiful."

"Off." Hope yanked at his sweatshirt.

He happily obliged. The garment went over his head quickly. Bare skin met bare skin, and he stroked his hands down her naked back.

I. Need. Her.

Jason lay back and took Hope with him. He flipped her onto her back, her body trapped beneath him; her legs wrapped around his waist. His cock throbbed as he looked at her face, her hair spread out wildly on the carpet, her eyes dark with passion.

"Jason, I—"

He thought he saw a flash of fear in her eyes as he covered her mouth with his finger to silence her. "Don't speak, Hope. Don't say no unless you really don't want this." He knew she did. She burned just as hotly as he did right now. He eased down and undid the button of her jeans, slid the zipper down and sat up to pull them down her shapely legs. Her panties went with them. "I have to taste you," he rasped, needing to watch her go over the edge.

"How?" she whispered urgently.

Jason hovered above her. Her eyes lit up with anticipation and… confusion? "Christ. Haven't you ever made love in any other way except fucking?" Her boyfriend must have been a jackass. How could he not have wanted to savor Hope?

"No," she admitted softly. "Not really."

"I'll show you." His voice was graveled with desire, desperate to pleasure her now that he knew he was going to be the first man to make her come this way.

Hope's nude body laid out on the cream-colored carpet in the firelight was a sight that Jason knew would be burned into his brain forever. She looked like something straight out of his fantasies. No… she looked even better.

I've never even imagined her quite like this.

Not even as the star of every one of his wet dreams had he pictured her like this. Jason knew exactly what he wanted to do: he wanted to make her come until she was spoiled for any other man. Fuck knew he was completely gone, and he wanted her to be just as desperate only for him as he was solely for her. If he was being avaricious and greedy, he didn't give a shit. He had to feel Hope's hunger for him.

He lowered his head to her breast and sucked her nipple into his mouth as his fingers teased her other breast.

"Jason." Hope moaned and speared her hands through his hair to bring his mouth harder against her breast.

The moment she moaned his name in pleasure, Jason knew he was completely lost in his fucking fantasy, and he had no desire to be found anytime soon. His control was gone, stripped from him by the needy, throaty sound of his name on Hope's lips. Jason tenaciously went after what he wanted, his mind focused on the only woman who could make him lose himself completely.

Chapter 3

Hope knew her body had won the war between her mind and her desire. Her need for Jason was so strong that she couldn't fight it anymore; she didn't even want to engage in emotional combat over it. She simply wanted to devour him whole, which she'd almost done when she'd jumped him. Desperately needing to feel connected to him, wanting to feel more of her burgeoning sensual desires, she'd responded with her instincts, and every part of her wanted this to happen with Jason.

One night. I just want this one night with him.

She hadn't wanted to explain the reason for her inexperience, and luckily, Jason hadn't pushed it. Now, she took what he offered. He made her body come to vibrant life, and all she wanted to do was feel.

Maybe with Jason, it's possible. This is new. I've never wanted a man this way.

She'd watched him as his eyes had devoured her nude body. There was no mistaking the hunger in his gaze, even though her body wasn't perfect, and Hope wanted to be the one to satiate this beautiful man, experience his passion and her own.

He finally lowered his head and a spiral of heat unfurled from her belly as his mouth covered her nipple, and his fingers played over her other breast.

"Jason," she moaned, needing him closer. Her fingers invaded his hair, latched onto his scalp, and brought his mouth harder against her breast. Liquid heat sizzled between her thighs. The attention he gave her breasts shot straight down to her core.

He bit gently at the tightened peaks of her breasts, one after the other, and then eased the sting with his tongue, driving her need higher. She shivered as his hand splayed over her abdomen and drifted down to slip a finger between her wet folds. Finally, he teased her clit, traveled around the needy bud in frustrating, sublime circles.

"You're so wet," Jason growled against her breast. His mouth moved down her belly. "I have to taste you."

Hope had never had a man go down on her before, and her pussy quivered with anticipation. He'd startled her when he'd talked about tasting her. She wasn't totally naïve, and it wasn't as if she hadn't heard women talk, but she had just started to understand real carnal need for herself. Apparently, firsthand experience was way different from learning clinically.

This is Jason, the man I've fantasized about since I was eighteen.

But this was better than any fantasy. He was hot, he was hard, and he was here. He parted her thighs with his broad shoulders and flicked his tongue over her lower abdomen lazily.

"Jason, please," she begged. Her hands tightened on his scalp and she tried to push his mouth down to where she really needed it as her body squirmed.

He moved, and the first touch of his tongue on the sensitive flesh between her thighs nearly made Hope go through the ceiling. Jason didn't just taste her; he feasted and groaned into her pussy as if he consumed a delicious forbidden fruit. Hope's body caught fire, and her back arched off the carpet in ecstasy. "Yes," she hissed as his tongue rolled over her clit, back and forth, and then circled the pulsating nub until she thought she'd go insane. "Oh, God. So good. So good," she whimpered. Her back eased down so she could lift her hips in a plea for relief from the heat that engulfed her, overwhelmed her.

Hope's head thrashed on the carpet; her body quivered as Jason caught her clit between his teeth lightly and increased the speed and pressure of the strokes of his tongue.

"Oh, God. Jason. I can't stand this," she keened as white-hot waves of heat exploded from her belly and pulsated to her core. Her climax hit her hard and rocked her body as she moaned, "Jason, Jason."

Her body went limp, spent, as she panted for air, her body slick with sweat. She released her death grip on his hair and let her hands drop to the side of her head.

Dear God. What Jason had done to her body left her stripped bare and feeling vulnerable. It had been breathtaking, but almost alarming. She had relinquished complete control of her body to him, and he'd pleasured her like it was his only mission in life. His strong-willed intensity had been too powerful to resist.

He crawled up her body. His big, powerful form trapped her beneath him. Jason had a muscular, sculpted body that had made her breath hitch as he'd pulled off his sweatshirt.

Jason kissed her, and she tasted herself on his lips. Her flavor mingled with his, and her core clenched with a need so overwhelming that she moaned into his mouth.

He pulled his mouth away from hers with a strangled groan; he went to his knees between her legs to yank at the buttons of his jeans. Hope watched his muscles flex; his abdomen and chest was exquisitely chiseled, perfectly defined.

"You're beautiful," Hope told him reverently. "I want to touch you." She sat up and eased his hands away from his jeans. "Let me do it." She wanted her hands and lips all over his golden skin.

"I'm not beautiful," he grunted. "And if you touch me, I'll lose control."

Hope wanted to see *that.* She wanted to see this gorgeous man splinter and come apart like she had just done. Her hands wandered over his biceps and to his chest. She savored the feel of his warm skin over hard muscle beneath her fingertips as she explored his six-pack abs. She buried her face against his chest and inhaled. His scent intoxicated her. Her tongue flicked out; she tasted his skin, laving one of his nipples as she fumbled with the buttons on his jeans. Regrettably, she had to move back to pop the rest of the buttons. "Stand," she requested huskily, needing to pull the jeans from his body.

Jason got up and Hope went to her knees. She lowered the denim that covered his lower body and took a pair of black briefs along with them. The breath left her lungs in a *whoosh* of astonishment as his cock sprang free.

Oh. My.

Jason kicked the pants and briefs off his legs, leaving them in a pile next to his feet.

Hope's eyes widened as she stared directly at his cock, her eyes level with the engorged member that bumped against his lower abdomen.

It's...enormous. It's going to hurt.

She had a moment of panic as she took in the length and girth of him.

It's Jason. Remember, it's Jason.

She lifted her hand and wrapped it around his cock, fascinated by the velvety feel of the skin over a surface that was so hard. The head glistened, and she flicked her tongue out to catch the small drop of moisture that was beaded at the top. He tasted like sin and lust. She wanted more.

"Hope. Don't." Jason's voice was urgent, his words a strangled groan.

He might be trying to warn her off, but Hope could tell he wanted more, too. His hands threaded into her hair as she stroked the tip of his cock with her tongue.

"Fuck," Jason rasped. "I'll come, Hope."

Like that was a bad thing? He brought me to an incredible climax with his mouth, and I want him to feel the same way.

Emboldened at the anguished sound of his voice, she took him deeper and sucked in as much of his length as she could, before she pulled back again. She'd never given head before either, but she knew how it was done. Her hand wrapped around the root of him, she used her mouth and hand in tandem, getting lost in the scent and taste of him.

Jason fisted her hair and groaned; he controlled her speed, urged her faster. Hope took action from his cues, the way his body and mind reacted.

Hope moved her eyes up to watch his face; it was important for her to see him. Jason looked down at her. His eyes were a swirling sea of carnal desire, covetous and possessive as they stayed riveted on what she did to him. Their eyes locked and held. Hope never slowed her pace as she willed him to come unraveled.

He did, and in glorious abandon. She watched as their eyes broke contact and he threw his head back. The corded muscles in his neck flexed as he let out a groan that could only be described as both agony and ecstasy.

His cock pulsated in her mouth, and Jason let go of her hair so she could escape his impending orgasm. But that wasn't what she wanted. She wanted to feel it, taste it on her tongue, experience it with him just like he'd experienced her climax with her. His hot release exploded into the back of her throat, and she swallowed, licked at the head and the shaft of his cock. She wanted every drop she could get from Jason.

He dropped to his knees, his chest heaving. Jason looked into her eyes and Hope felt herself drown in a brooding sea of emotion.

"Jesus, woman. You nearly killed me," Jason grumbled, his breathing still laborious.

She lifted her hand to his jaw and stroked over his whiskered cheek. "You look like you lived through it."

"Just barely," he grunted. "I knew that beautiful mouth was dangerous."

She laughed as he took her down to the carpet. His body loomed over hers as he kissed her.

His mouth moved from her lips to her neck, his face buried in her hair. "Hope," he muttered gutturally. His strong hands wrapped around her wrists and restrained them over her head.

She pulled at her wrists, unable to get free of his grip.

This is Jason. Don't panic.

Her heart raced, and the feeling of being under Jason's control aroused her body, but her brain rebelled. Foggy images took over her mind, and she was suddenly in another place:

Her wrists restrained, her body helpless to fight against someone much bigger, stronger.

Invaded, and so much pain: a sharp, excruciating lance between her thighs that burned and burned and burned.

Her own screams echoing through the room, but nobody coming to help her.

Please, let it be over. Let it be over.

Terror consumed her, and Hope felt a scream rise in her throat. Frantically, she jerked at her wrists until Jason finally let go, and she pushed against his shoulders, desperate to get free.

I can't do it, no matter how badly I want Jason. I can't do it.

Jason rose to his knees, took his weight from her body and looked down at her with a puzzled expression. "Are you okay?"

No. I'm not okay. I'm broken. I want you so desperately, but I'm not capable of taking the final step.

Her breath sawed in and out of her lungs, her heart raced frantically, and her body shook with fright. Her mind cleared slowly, and she looked up at the man she wanted so desperately. *Jason.* He'd given her the most intense pleasure she'd ever known, and she knew she'd pleasured his body, but she couldn't give herself to him completely. She couldn't give herself totally to anyone.

"I'm not ready, Jason," she told him nervously. Disappointment hit her in pummeling waves, and she wrapped her arms around her waist. The emotional agony consumed her.

He pulled her quivering, nude body into his lap. "Too soon after your ex-boyfriend?" He sounded concerned and irritated at the same time.

He wrapped his arms around her and she laid her head on his shoulder. "Yes." The excuse was as good as any, even if it wasn't true. Tears leaked from her eyes, and she closed them, her heart full of pain.

She'd hoped.

She'd wanted.

She'd tried because it was Jason, and she wanted him so damn badly.

So far...she had come so far, so close...

"Hey." He pulled back and took her head between his hands to force her to look at him. "It's okay." Gently, he swiped at her tears. "I can wait."

Don't wait. I'll never be whole again. I thought I would, but obviously I can't. I can never give you what you want. If I can't experience this with you, I can't do it with anyone.

"It will be a long wait," she tried to dissuade him.

He picked her up and stood, cradled her naked body in his arms. Hope wrapped her arms around his neck and savored the feel of his heated skin against hers as he carried her up the stairs and to her bedroom. He turned the covers back, dropped her gently on the bed and crawled in beside her. "Just sleep with me then." He pulled the sheet and blanket over them and enveloped them in a cocoon where only the two of them existed. His arms tightened around her and pulled her half on top of him.

"Yes." All the tension drained out of Hope's body as she inhaled his distinctive scent. She was safe with Jason. "Just for tonight." She wanted this intimate connection with Jason. He felt so good. Smelled so good. The comforting stroke of his hands in her hair, up and down the bare skin of her back, lulled her into a sense of well-being she'd never known.

"For *now*," he corrected huskily, gently.

Hope sighed and threaded her fingers through his hair. They fell asleep just like that, molded together, wrapped up in the comfort of each other's touch.

She'd just left. No note, no goodbye. She was just gone like she'd never been there.

Jason sat down in a comfortable leather seat on his private jet and pulled out his laptop, pissed off and angry because he'd woken up this morning and Hope had already left. He hadn't heard a word from any of her brothers, who would have been irate if they'd seen his rental car at her house. Obviously, she hadn't allowed them to see it, had probably walked to the end of her driveway when they had picked her up this morning just to avoid it.

Evan's jet had already departed a few hours before Jason had woken up at noon, and he'd known the minute he saw the time and the empty space beside him that Hope was gone. Evan had mentioned that he was leaving by ten, and Jason had known that Hope would be on that plane.

Fuck! She could have at least said goodbye.

Jason held the key he'd found on the kitchen table between his thumb and index finger, staring at it intently before dropping it into the pocket of his buttoned-down shirt. Whether or not she'd intentionally left the key to her house there for him or not he didn't know. But he'd used it to lock up before he left, and he was keeping it.

He'd give her time, but he and Hope weren't finished. He wouldn't allow it. She could run…for now.

I'm not ready.

Her words echoed in his brain, over and over. It hadn't mattered that he hadn't actually fucked her. Just the feel of her lips on his bare skin, her beautiful mouth on his cock had been enough to completely turn him upside down. Just being with Hope had temporarily soothed his loneliness, cured the restlessness that had plagued him for a very long time. Last night had been a revelation for him. Thinking back on all the meaningless relationships he'd had over the last eight years, since the moment he'd seen her again at her high school graduation, he now knew one thing for certain:

I've always been biding my time, waiting for Hope.

His anger fled, replaced by concern as he thought about the night before, the broken look on her face when she'd told him she wasn't ready. He could have sworn he saw a flash of worry, a moment of fear in her eyes. Had he imagined things, or had she really been afraid? Most likely, he was imagining it. Hope had had boyfriends before, the most recent one for several years, a deadbeat who had no job, and was obviously a selfish bastard judging by Hope's lack of sensual experience.

He just fucked her and sponged off her.

That thought made Jason insane. Hope had a huge heart, and he didn't like the thought of anyone taking advantage of her.

His fingers flew over the keyboard of his laptop and accessed his private email. Searching, he finally found the email Grady had sent to everyone when he'd become engaged. He found her name among the group and he started a new email with her address:

I need to know you made it home safe and that you're okay. If I don't hear from you, I'll find you.

J.

He pressed the *Send* button harder than necessary.

Her response came that evening, when Jason was home in his New York penthouse:

I'm back in Aspen, and I'm okay.

H.

Leaning back in the desk chair of his home office, he closed his eyes. Dammit. He'd wanted further information. Yes, he wanted to know she was safe, but he'd wanted her to say more, tell him more, let him know how she felt.

Holy shit! He started to sound like a woman, wanting to pry Hope's emotions from her until she talked. Usually, he avoided emotional confrontations at all costs. He was an only child, so he didn't have sisters who tried to strangle him with emotional bullshit. And if a woman started to even begin to show an emotional attachment, he was done with the relationship. Most times, he didn't have to worry about it. He was careful, stuck to women who just wanted or needed sex with no strings, and that had worked out well for him most of the time.

I'm losing it.

Hope Sinclair would come with all kinds of strings attached, and she'd already tied some of the knots to secure them to him. Strangely, he didn't give a shit. Casual sex was going to be a thing of the past. She'd ruined him. And if he had to wait...he'd wait. Hell, he'd already waited eight years for her to grow up. Now, he wished he hadn't waited so damn long.

She's mine. She's always been mine.

Eventually, he'd snare Hope Sinclair, and keep her until they had both fucked each other out of their systems. It was the only way he could think of to get his sanity back again.

Maybe then I'll be able to concentrate. Maybe the restlessness and loneliness will go away if I have Hope as many times as we both want it.

He deleted her email and brought up his work documents, with a fervent hope he didn't have to wait too damn long.

For the next several months, Jason tried to give Hope a chance to recover from her relationship with her loser boyfriend, tried to be patient.

Unfortunately, he couldn't seem to stop emailing her at least once a week. He wanted to know whether she was doing okay, and some secret part of him did it for completely selfish reasons: to remind her that he was waiting. The emails he sent were always the same:

I just want to know that you're doing okay.

J.

Her answers were always two words:

I'm fine.

H.

In January when he emailed, she was *fine.*

For the rest of the winter when he wrote, she was *fine.*

In the spring, she answered his query the same way: she was *fine.*

Then, in the early summer, she was *getting married.*

What. The. Fuck.

Jason was in Rocky Springs, Colorado, at a charity benefit function when he found out that Hope planned to marry the same loser who Jason was waiting for her to get over. He'd talked to her brother, Grady, and had gotten the news from him. Hope had never mentioned it. She was just *fine*, according to her weekly, two-word email responses.

She'd never let him know that she was back with her ex-boyfriend, much less that they were getting married.

Unfortunately, *Jason* wasn't so *fine* with the news. He was fucking livid, and he'd had enough of waiting.

He was finally going to get Hope in his bed and oust the asshole in her life when he did; he wasn't opposed to playing dirty if that's what it took to achieve his goal. Jason didn't know what kind of number this guy was doing on Hope to get her to marry him, but the game was about to end.

Unfortunately, even though she had plans to marry another man, a guy who didn't give a rat's ass about her, Jason still wanted her for himself. And he wasn't giving her up until he was damn good and ready to do so, and the asshole in her life was completely out of the picture. For some reason, she was running away from what had happened between them, but he'd catch her, make her admit she wanted him and didn't love the man she was marrying. If she had loved another man, she never would have been intimate with him at the holidays.

Maybe Hope thought Jason was only an asshole on the surface, but she was about to find out just how big of an asshole he could really be. When it came to Hope, he was perfectly capable of being a ruthless bastard to have her, keep her away from someone who would hurt her, and she was about to see a different side of him. So, she could end up hating him. It was better than her ending up married and miserable, tied to a bloodsucker.

He and Tate Colter, a half-crazy, very wealthy ex-Special Forces guy, put together a plan in Rocky Springs, right after Jason found out that Hope was getting married. It was a selfish, greedy scheme that would change his life and Hope's irrevocably. Jason didn't think twice about implementing it with Tate's help. His reason clouded with anger and disbelief, he plowed ahead with Tate, his only objective to separate Hope from any other man except him. Any other outcome was unacceptable, unthinkable.

Jason ignored the niggling voice that told him that ending her marriage plans wasn't the only reason he was taking this particular strategy. Instead, he set the plan in motion, eventually slamming a barrier between himself and any of his emotions after he'd made the decision to act out Tate's proposed solution, just like he'd always done in business. He and Hope *did* have unfinished business, and he was about to wrap it up—permanently and completely.

Billionaire
Unmasked

J.S. SCOTT

Chapter 1

Rocky Springs, Colorado – The Present

"Is she still out cold?" Tate Colter asked curiously as Jason walked back into the living room of one of the guesthouses in Tate's Rocky Springs, Colorado resort.

Jason had met the obscenely wealthy Tate Colter at a charity event here in Rocky Springs, and he'd been here at the charity event Colter had hosted when he'd heard that Hope was getting married. Tate had been the one to come up with this whole crazy plan in the first place, and helped coordinate everything. As an ex-Special Forces guy, Colter was more precise at executing a plan and more calculating than Jason when it came to deception.

Jason looked over at Tate. He frowned as he noticed that Tate was on Hope's laptop, his ass planted in a comfortable recliner. "What are you doing?"

"Getting all the dirt on your woman," Tate replied unremorsefully. "It's amazing how much a person can learn about someone by looking at their computer."

Jason raised his eyebrows. "You hacked into her computer?"

Tate shrugged. "It wasn't difficult. She needs better security. But that still wouldn't have prevented me from getting in." He grinned shamelessly at Jason.

Jason felt a twinge of guilt, but he shrugged it off. "Get out of her personal stuff," he growled at Tate. It annoyed the hell out of him that Tate saw anything personal about Hope.

"Nothing's personal if it's on a computer. You gotta see some of this stuff." Tate's gaze went back to the computer screen. "Did you know she was a photographer? And not just *any* photographer. She does radical stuff." His voice was slightly awed. "She might be crazier than I am."

Jason doubted that, although he was pretty sure he needed his own head examined because of what had happened over the last twenty-four hours.

When Grady had told him that Hope was getting married and she was currently in Vegas for a bachelorette party, Jason had flown to Vegas to intentionally track her down, like some kind of mad stalker. She hadn't been difficult to find, and after he'd gotten her room number in the hotel she was staying in, he'd followed her, pretended he was there on business. But the meeting had been far from accidental. He'd gritted his teeth as he congratulated her on her upcoming marriage—the words nearly killed him as he said them—and dragged her out for celebratory drinks. She'd fell right into his plan, became pretty damn intoxicated very quickly, and threw caution to the wind by the time she'd had just a couple of drinks. She'd just gotten more and more toasted with every subsequent drink. Obviously Hope didn't hold her liquor well. She had passed out somewhere over Colorado on the flight back, and Jason had carried her into the bedroom of the guesthouse here in Rocky Springs. It was the same guesthouse he'd stayed in when he'd left for Vegas. It had been Colter's idea to bring her here, to make it more difficult for her to leave. She was a good five-hour drive from Aspen, and she didn't have a car. It was unlikely they'd encounter another person considering they were on private Colter land; the town of Rocky Springs was several miles away.

Tate's whistle of appreciation drew Jason from his thoughts.

"Let me see that." Jason grabbed the laptop from Tate and planted his butt in another recliner, determined to see what had Tate Colter so damn impressed. Not to mention the fact that he wanted to prevent Colter from looking at any more of Hope's private life.

He looked through the photo gallery at some of the pictures Tate had ogled, stunned by what he saw. The pictures were raw and beautiful in a frightening kind of way. Quite a few of them were of large tornados, taken from close proximity. The rest were all of some kind of extreme forces of nature, everything from twisters to gale force winds that nearly bent trees in half, probably hurricanes. "These can't be hers," Jason denied. He shuddered at the thought of Hope being close enough to take photos of something so damn dangerous.

"They're hers," Tate said in a cocky voice. "If you check her email, she has travel confirmations that coincide with the pictures. And she has an entire portfolio with her luggage that we got at the hotel. The photos have her marking in the bottom right corner. I'm assuming she's H.L. Sinclair. I did a search on the name. She's idolized in the photography world as an extreme weather photographer. Hell, she sounds more like my kind of woman than yours." Tate grinned at Jason. "She must have some balls to be traveling to every corner of the world for that kind of shit."

"She doesn't have balls," Jason snarled as he looked through all of the pictures that Hope had apparently taken. "Jesus Christ. What in the hell has she been doing?"

"Taking photos, apparently. She got a degree in fine arts with an emphasis on photography. I saw it in her biography."

Jason scowled at the computer screen. He'd known she'd gotten a degree in fine arts, but he *hadn't* known she was a photographer, and now it pissed him off that Tate knew more about Hope than he did. Why hadn't he known? Maybe it was because he'd spent years trying to control himself around her, used every ounce of willpower he had not to toss her over his shoulder and take her away somewhere, anywhere with him. "I guarantee her brothers don't know.

They would have locked her up and thrown away the key if they'd known she was doing this shit."

"That's probably why she never told them," Tate mused philosophically. "She's a grown adult, man. She can do whatever she wants."

"Not this," Jason replied angrily. "She can't be traipsing around the world, throwing herself into danger." Every hair on his body stood up in alarm as he viewed some pictures of what was a hurricane, typhoon, or cyclone. It was hard to tell where the photos had been taken. All Jason knew was that Hope had to have been sheltering there *during* the damn storm. She had captured the shot just as a roof was torn from a building, the picture horrifying evidence of the violence of the tempest she'd thrown herself into.

"Of course she can go. She's a grown woman," Tate argued reasonably.

Jason wasn't feeling reasonable. "She's mine now," he snapped back at Tate.

"She wasn't yours when she took the pictures, and you snatched her out of Vegas, not knowing who she really is *now*. You've seen her what—a handful of times as an adult? You can't expect her to stop her life because she got drunk and followed you here willingly just because she was three sheets to the wind."

Selfishly, that was exactly what Jason wanted. He'd taken her with the intention of sating himself with her, before eventually letting her go. Already angry and hurt that she hadn't told him that she was getting married, all he'd wanted was Hope in his bed, and to prevent her from marrying an asshole. Now he wasn't so sure he was going to let her out of his sight ever again. Not that he wasn't *still* pissed off at her, but his protective instincts overrode his anger. Jesus, did she have some sort of death wish to be chasing these kind of storms?

You don't know me anymore.

Hope had told him that when they'd been together in Amesport. Turns out...she was right. "She has an entire secret life that nobody knows about," Jason speculated aloud, pissed off and troubled. Where in the hell was the shy girl he had known, the quiet, sweet young woman he'd seen right before she left for college? Every time he'd seen her after that fateful day, she'd been quiet and subdued, doing nothing to indicate that she'd…changed.

"We all have our secrets," Tate said solemnly. "She's accomplished a lot for a woman her age. She sells a lot of her photos to major publications, and she's already highly respected in her field."

"It's fucking dangerous," Jason replied irritably. "How would you feel if you cared about someone who rushed into dangerous situations all the time? What if it was your sister, Chloe?"

Tate frowned. "I'd lock her up and throw away the key."

Jason raised his eyebrows, giving Tate an I-told-you-so stare.

"She's my little sister," Tate continued defensively.

"Exactly. Someone you care about, someone you want to protect."

"She's related," Tate grumbled. "I've never felt that way about any woman. I couldn't. I did some crazy shit. On any given mission, there was always a very good chance that when I left, I wouldn't be coming back."

Jason watched Tate's face, the brief, haunted look that flashed in his eyes. He wasn't Special Forces anymore, but some things Tate had done during his military days obviously still preyed on his mind. "You're loaded, Colter. You have a good family. Why did you do it?" Jason wondered why someone with Tate's privileged background would join Special Forces. In fact, Tate was the only billionaire he knew who had even enlisted in the military when they had billions of dollars in the bank.

Tate shrugged. "Because I could. I'm a damn good pilot, and I thrived on the adrenaline for a long time. We did some good things, saved some lives. It was worth it."

Tate could be an annoyingly arrogant son of a bitch, but Jason respected him. No doubt he *had* saved lives. "You're not in Special Forces anymore. What's the excuse for not having a woman now?"

"What was yours?" Tate shot back at Jason.

"I was obsessed with Hope," Jason admitted readily. His fixation with Hope had always been in the back of his mind every time he was with a woman. Hopefully, he could fuck that fascination away now that he had her. They'd probably be sick of each other after a day or two together.

Tate squirmed. "Yeah. Well, I guess I just haven't found a woman worth obsessing over. Thank God," he mumbled in a low, fervent voice.

Jason ran a frustrated hand through his hair. "Maybe that's not such a bad thing." His mind was blurry from lack of sleep, and his head spun from finding out so much about Hope that he hadn't known. Maybe finding everything out now was a good thing. Maybe the fact that she was obviously a compulsive liar and not the sweet woman he thought he knew would cure him of his compulsion to fuck her, make her his. He sure as hell hoped it would. Unfortunately, even though he was pissed, his protective instincts were still present and even stronger now that he knew she ran into danger all the time. Regrettably, he also knew the Hope he had known was still there. He'd sampled her sweetness on their one night together over the holidays, and that taste of her had just left an agonizing desire for more.

I don't know who she is now.

"Get some rest." Tate got up from the recliner. "Do you need anything else?"

"I have to find a way to get Hope's cat," Jason answered with a grimace. "Hope was only planning to be gone for a few days. I don't know if anyone is taking care of her cat."

"I'll deal with it," Tate replied nonchalantly. "I'll drop the cat off later. It's a short helicopter ride." He strode to the door and opened it.

"Tate?" Jason raised his voice so Tate could hear him across the room.

"Yeah?"

"Don't you want her address?"

Tate smirked. "I hacked her computer. I have it."

"Keys to her condo?"

"I've never met a lock I couldn't pick," Tate told Jason arrogantly. "Later." He closed the door behind him.

"Cocky bastard," Jason grumbled as he went to the door Tate had just exited and locked it, although he was actually more angry with himself than he was at Tate. Colter had actually helped him reach an objective: stop Hope from marrying somebody else, a man who, most likely, cared nothing about her and had to have been sponging off Hope for years if he'd never gotten a job. His other reasons were connected to his main objective and were just as urgent, but purely selfish.

Jason tried to pacify his guilt by telling himself that Hope would end up happier in the long run, but that didn't help him now. That damn, niggling voice inside his head was back, and he couldn't seem to quite close the door on his emotions entirely. Granted, the voice wasn't loud enough to stop him from doing what he needed to do, but it was annoying to have some regrets about basically kidnapping Hope, even if she had gone with him willingly, albeit completely intoxicated.

He sat back down with her computer, unable to stop himself from perusing every bit of data he could find. Tate had left the computer open, and seeking out information on Hope was just too big of a temptation. Desperate to piece together her life, he tried to fit all of the data together. Some of it made sense; much of it didn't.

She had a lot of emails from a guy named David. Was this the mysterious fiancé? *I don't even know the guy's name!* Although, most of the emails exchanged were nothing more than meeting sites and travel plans. There was nothing romantic, and very little personal information exchanged. David was apparently in Oklahoma, from what Jason could surmise.

Curious, he Googled her *H.L. Sinclair* persona just like Tate had done, and came to the same conclusion as Tate: she was a very well-respected photographer who specialized in extreme weather photography. Hope even had a website, but there wasn't a single picture of herself. Every photo was of violent storms or the aftermath.

Jesus. How does Hope cope with that kind of suffering and pain?

Hope was the kind of woman who would shelter a deaf cat because she couldn't bear to see the animal suffer. How did she deal with human tragedy on this scale?

In some of the photos, he saw the same man—a dark, tall, young guy, probably around Hope's age. He was usually in the thick of these disasters, just like the woman who took the pictures.

"Her fiancé?" he asked himself in a disgusted voice. Hell, he didn't even know the name of her intended, and that annoyed him. He should at least know the guy's name, right?

Irritated, Jason dug out his cell phone and punched in Grady's number.

"What's the name of Hope's fiancé?" Jason asked after Grady had said hello, without any of the usual bullshit they usually exchanged.

"She always just referred to him as James. I asked her his last name once and she said it was Smith," Grady grumbled. "If you're going to try to check him out, forget it. I already tried. Do you know how common that name is in Colorado? Without an occupation or any other identifying information, I can't be certain exactly which James Smith is taking advantage of my little sister," Grady admitted gruffly.

"Shit," Jason snapped fractiously. "Do they live together? Is he in Aspen?"

"Don't know. Hope always says it's none of my business. She never wants to talk about him. The only thing she said when I talked to her was that they were working their problems out and that they were getting married. Then she told me she was going to Vegas for a few days with friends for a bachelorette party. Short of having her followed, I can't get the damn information out of her. And believe me, I've thought about putting a tail on her. But if she ever found out, she'd be really hurt. She lives a quiet life in Aspen, and she's never wanted to be in the media or bring attention to herself." Grady sighed. "All of us have threatened to go there to meet the guy, but Hope promised she'd bring him to Amesport or we'd all meet somewhere before she marries him. She hasn't even set a date yet, so I didn't push her. She sounded wiped out the day she told me. Said she was tired."

Jason came very close to outing himself, telling Grady exactly what he'd done, but he didn't. If Grady knew he'd found his little sister in Vegas, and then got her so inebriated that she didn't know what she was doing, he'd kick his ass. Jason wasn't worried about paying for what he'd done. In fact, he expected it. He just didn't want to let the cat out of the bag too soon. He needed time with Hope first. "I was thinking about checking him out after you told me she was marrying him. I'm worried about her marrying a guy nobody knows," Jason admitted, worried more now than he ever had been before. Hope wasn't living the quiet life in Aspen that Grady thought she was—not even close.

"I didn't know you two really kept in touch," Grady said thoughtfully.

"We don't connect as often as I'd like," Jason confessed. "Since your engagement party on New Year's, we email each other, but I've always considered her a friend." Jason nearly choked on the word *friend.* And "emailing" was a stretch. He sent a short sentence every week and she emailed back the same two words.

I'm fine.

"Damn nice of you to care enough to worry," Grady said in a low, genuine voice.

Jason really started to suffocate from guilt. He only gave a shit because he was a selfish bastard, not out of the goodness of his heart. "I care," he answered huskily. At least that statement was true, no matter his motives. "So how's Emily doing?" Jason asked curiously.

Grady perked up immediately and started to wax poetic about his wife. Jason smiled as his friend went on and on about how much Emily had changed his life. Obviously there were no problems in *that* particular marriage. Grady adored Emily, and worried about her obsessively. Even though Jason had never wanted that kind of attachment to a woman, he almost envied Grady. He was happy, and the man had changed, and definitely for the better since Emily had come into his life. Once a lonely recluse, Grady was now practically worshipped by the entire town of Amesport, Maine. There was no doubt in Jason's mind that Emily loved Grady just as intensely as he loved her. He'd seen it in her eyes when Jason had seen them together during the holidays.

Unfortunately, he hadn't been able to make it to their wedding. It had come at a time when he absolutely had to be in London on business, and Grady had made sure he married Emily with very little planning, as if he was afraid Emily would change her mind. At the time, Jason hadn't been sure whether that previous commitment had been a blessing or a curse. He'd wanted to see Hope so damn desperately, but he wasn't certain he would have been able to hide the fact that he wanted to fuck her if he saw her again. Honestly, he wasn't certain he wouldn't have thrown her over his shoulder and boarded his jet with her in tow, taking her anywhere that they could be alone together.

He talked to Grady for another thirty minutes, mostly about Emily, and Grady's brothers. By the time he hung up, Jason almost saw double and his body begged for sleep.

He wandered into the bedroom and he immediately got hard when he saw Hope in the bed, her fiery hair splashed over a snowy white pillow. Obviously his dick was the only part of him *not* exhausted, and that part of his anatomy wasn't angry with Hope at all. Even passed out on the bed, Hope looked breathtakingly beautiful. He'd pulled off her sandals, but he'd left her dressed in a pair of shorts and her tank top.

There's only so much torture a guy can take!

He wasn't about to fondle Hope while she was inebriated or unconscious. He wanted her awake and aware of everything that was happening when he buried himself inside her for the first time. And he'd be doing exactly that very soon.

Mine.

Jason wrestled with his sense of honor and morals again, wondered whether every man had a moment in his life where he'd do anything to get something or someone he wanted. This was a first for him. Admittedly, he took business risks, but only after he'd carefully calculated the risks and benefits of taking a particular action, when he was fairly certain of getting his expected outcome. He'd rushed into the last twenty-four hours strictly from emotion and lust, not bothering to even consider the consequences.

I'm just that pathetic and desperate to have her in my bed.

What the hell was happening to him? He could argue with himself forever, rationalize the reasons he'd done what he did, but it all came down to selfishness. He wanted Hope.

What the hell does it matter? It's not like I'm keeping her forever. We're going to have sex every day, every hour, until we're both satisfied and tired of each other. When I know she isn't going to marry the loser, and I have her out of my system, we can end this little unplanned vacation.

Jason scowled; his mind and body rebelled at that thought for some reason. His possessive instincts surged through his body as he gazed at her, so innocent and vulnerable as she slept.

Mine.

Now that he knew some of her secrets and was aware of how she'd lied to everyone to keep them, he felt even more protective of her, needed to keep her safe, even though he was so angry he wanted to wake her up and shake her to tell him the whole truth. And why she'd lied.

He forced himself not to look at Hope anymore, shucked off his pants and shirt and closed the shutters on the windows to dim the light. It was late in the afternoon, but the room was still bright.

He climbed into the bed beside her and smiled as he wondered whether she made that delicate snoring sound when she wasn't intoxicated. It was actually kind of...sexy.

She moaned and rolled over on her side. Her hands immediately reached for him and she draped her body over his like a heat-seeking missile. "Jason," she whispered with a low, sleepy voice full of intense longing.

She wasn't awake, so he wondered how she knew it was him and not her fiancé.

She's searching for me in her bed.

The fact that she looked for him, sought him out subconsciously, hit him in the gut like a sucker punch. He wrapped his arms around her protectively.

"You've got a lot to answer for, woman," he whispered roughly. His eyes closed, and he felt as if Hope was finally exactly where she was supposed to be. His dick was hard, but he was content not to act on that. Right now, it was enough to know she was here, and that he might finally get free of his long, horny preoccupation with her.

Not wanting to think about later, and with Hope's warm body half covering his, he closed his eyes and slept.

Chapter 2

H ope woke up slowly. Her head pounded as if someone slung a hammer at her skull. Her stomach roiled with nausea. The light hurt her eyes and she closed them again; one hand went to her aching head and the other to her rebellious stomach.

What the hell had happened?

Desperate to use the bathroom—her bladder felt as if it was about to explode—she opened her eyes carefully to let the light seep in gradually.

Oh, shit.

Eventually, her eyes adjusted to the dim light, and she became aware of a very large, very warm body next to hers. She jerked her head toward the form lying beside her, and moaned from the pain of moving so quickly and the exact identity of the unyielding mass of muscle next to her.

Jason?

Where in the hell am I?

Hope inched out of the bed slowly, determined to find the bathroom. She didn't have to look far. There was one attached to this bedroom, so close that she could see it. As she sat up on the edge of the bed, her head pounding, the short distance to the visible toilet across the room seemed like miles in her current condition.

Get up. Get there before you embarrass yourself.

"Need help?"

Hope flinched at the low, smooth baritone. While it was soft and gentle, right now, to her aching head, it sounded as if Jason screamed at her. "No," she responded, embarrassed, as her eyes focused on those awesome abs right in front of her. He'd gotten out of bed and stood in front of her without her even noticing. Jason was in a pair of navy boxer briefs and nothing else. Mortified, she couldn't even look him in the eyes.

Without a word, Jason picked her up and carted her to the bathroom, lowered her feet gently to the floor before he exited and closed the door without a word.

Thank God!

Hope took care of her body's urgent needs and managed to make it to the vanity, which she used to prop herself up as she washed her hands. Her head still spun. As she stood straight again, the room tilted.

A large, masculine arm popped through the door and dropped a modest nightgown into the bathroom. She stared at it, puddled on the floor, before she shakily sat herself on the toilet seat lid and reached for it. Taking off everything except her underwear, she lowered it over her head.

Her mouth as dry as the desert, she reached toward the vanity and grabbed one of the upside-down cups and filled it with water, not really caring whether the cup was clean or not. It was upside down, so she assumed it was unused. She drank the water slowly as she eyed the container full of packaged, new toothbrushes and the tube of toothpaste beside the sink. Putting one of them to use, she quickly cleaned her teeth, rinsed and then drank more water. Had she gotten sick? Right now, nothing made sense in her fuzzy brain except for the fact that she felt like crap.

Jason eased the door open, silently scooped her up, and took her back to the bed. After he handed her some pills that looked like ibuprofen, he gave her a bottle of Gatorade.

"Take those and have something to eat. You'll feel better," he said quietly.

She took the pills and swallowed them down with the sports drink, eying the tray in front of her dubiously. It was only a few slices of toast, but her stomach revolted at the thought of actually eating. "I don't think I can eat," she croaked. "Where are we?"

Jason reached for the toast, broke off a small piece, and held it to her mouth. "You need to get something in your stomach. Don't you remember Vegas?"

Vegas.

Meeting up with Jason by accident.

Panic.

Drinks.

More panic.

More drinks.

She obediently opened her mouth and absently took the bite Jason offered, and tried to sort out all of her jumbled thoughts as she chewed. The memories were foggy now, but she remembered how nervous she'd been, afraid Jason would discover the truth. She'd used alcohol for liquid courage, something she'd never done before in her entire life. She was a light drinker, careful because her father had been a raging alcoholic. Jason ridiculously fed her by hand and she accepted another piece of toast distractedly.

After she swallowed, she asked hesitantly, "Am I sick?"

"Hangover," Jason said mildly. "You were pretty wasted."

She'd never had a hangover, never drank enough to experience one. Right then and there, she swore she'd never have another one. She felt as if she'd been chewed up and spit out of a giant meat grinder. "I don't usually drink that much," she whispered softly.

"Welcome to the world of excessive partying," Jason answered mildly. "You need to go back to sleep. It's the best thing for you right now." He popped another piece of bread into her mouth.

Hope lifted her hand to indicate she'd had enough of the toast. Jason took the tray. "Finish the Gatorade. You're probably dehydrated." He left the bedroom, obviously to get rid of the tray.

Hope sipped slowly at the drink; her headache started to ease. As she looked around the mammoth, luxurious bedroom, she wondered what hotel he was staying at in Vegas. It was quite a place, and it didn't have the feel of even an upscale hotel.

The clock next to her bed read around seven a.m. "My flight," she murmured, alarmed. She had an early flight out of Vegas.

"Canceled," Jason said gruffly as he strolled back into the bedroom, looking completely at ease with being nearly naked.

A guy like him doesn't need to be self-conscious.

Jason was an earthbound Adonis, and just as overwhelmingly heart-stopping as the mythological figure was depicted to be.

"You canceled my flight?" she asked, astonished.

Jason replied ironically, "It certainly wasn't looking like you were going to be on it. They don't let excessively drunk people fly on commercial aircrafts," he answered noncommittally. "Sleep, Hope."

She drained the bottle of Gatorade and set it lightly on the nightstand, wishing she was certain she could make it to the kitchen to throw it in the trash, but she wasn't positive she could walk that far. Her eyes were heavy, and her head still ached. "I feel miserable. I'm sorry you got stuck taking care of me." She hated that she'd gotten so out of control that Jason had needed to babysit her. Apparently, she was staying with him, and he even slept in the same bed to watch out for her. Evidently, he didn't bother with pajamas. Maybe he actually slept in the nude, and he was being considerate by donning his briefs. She swallowed nervously at that thought as she tried not to picture his incredible, naked body deliciously tangled up in sheets while he was sleeping.

Jason slid into the bed and pulled her compliant body against his side, resting her head on his shoulder. "You'll feel better when you wake up." He paused before he added teasingly, "Maybe you won't snore this time."

"Did I snore?" Hope was mortified.

"You did. But it's kind of erotic," he answered. "Sort of like a loud, purring cat."

"I was drunk," she answered, disgruntled. Her eyes drifted closed.

Jason's soft chuckle was the last thing she heard before she floated back to sleep.

Hope woke up more aware of her surroundings, the ache in her head only a dull pain. Her nausea had calmed down and she was thirsty.

Jason's side of the bed was empty, the indented pillow the only indication that she hadn't had some wild dream about him being here earlier.

Three p.m.

The clock on the nightstand indicated that she'd slept the day away. "Holy shit," she whispered, still disoriented. She must have been completely wasted, although she couldn't remember how many drinks she'd had. Obviously too many! Her feet met the plush carpet as she slipped out of the bed, making her sigh quietly, nervously. How had she gotten herself so messed up? She went to the bathroom and drank some more water. As she entered the room again, she noticed her luggage stacked in a corner of the bedroom.

How did it get here? Had Jason needed to check her out of her room, and brought her and her luggage back to wherever he was staying?

She cringed as she saw her large portfolio next to her suitcase. Damning evidence. Was it possible he hadn't noticed?

Hope startled as she felt a familiar sensation: her feline brushed against her bare legs as Daisy moved around Hope in a welcoming circle. "Daisy?" She picked up her cat automatically.

What. The. Hell?

She opened the bedroom door and looked around at what she belatedly realized was definitely no hotel suite. Petting Daisy nervously, she walked down the hall, to a spacious living room with a fireplace and wooden beams that spanned a tall, cathedral ceiling off to the left. To the right was a beautiful cook's kitchen, with hanging copper pots and gleaming granite countertops.

"Incredible," she murmured. How had Jason scored a place like this in Las Vegas, even if he was a billionaire? He had to be staying off the Strip or outside of the city.

"You okay?" Jason rumbled from a recliner in the living room.

Hope hadn't seen him. She'd been too busy looking up at the ceiling. "Yeah. I think so." He looked good enough to eat in a pair of jeans and a buttoned-down shirt that matched his glorious blue eyes. "What are you doing? Where are we?"

Jason stood. "I was waiting for you to wake up." He tossed aside the laptop he'd been using and set it on the chair as he got up.

"I'm so sorry this happened. I never get drunk. I'm sorry you had to take care of me last night. I'll just shower and get out of your way. I'll catch the first flight I can get to Aspen."

"Not just last night," Jason informed her nonchalantly. "Hope, we met up two days ago at about this time."

"T-Two days?" she stammered. *Impossible.* "Oh, God. I have to get back to Colorado." She set Daisy on the floor shakily.

"You are back." Jason moved across the room to stand in front of her.

"In Aspen?"

"Rocky Springs," he answered abruptly.

Rocky Springs? Hope knew *of* the decadent, lush resort town, but she'd never been there. "Why am I here? Why is Daisy here?"

Jason shrugged. "My business was finished in Las Vegas. And the cat was brought here because I wasn't sure if anyone was taking care of her because you were delayed. The Colters, the family who owns this property, are friends. I had some business to discuss with Tate Colter, so I brought you with me."

She'd heard about the Colters. Everyone in Colorado knew about the obscenely rich family who owned just about everything in this area. "Okay." Hope blew out a pensive breath. "That will make it easier, I guess. At least I'm back. I take it I have you to thank for bringing me back to Colorado." He'd obviously hoisted her onto his private jet. She'd put him to enough trouble. It would be easy for her to get back to Aspen. "If you don't mind, I'll grab a shower and get out of your hair. I'm sure I can rent a car in town, but I might need a ride there." She turned on her heel to retreat, mortified that she'd lost so much control that she didn't remember two whole days out of her life.

She didn't make it very far. Jason grabbed her by her upper arm and swung her back around. "You're staying for a while," he informed her, his face impassive.

"I can't stay. I have obligations," she said irritably, not happy with his bossy tone.

"You're staying," Jason repeated. "And we're going to have a little talk. Then I'm taking you to bed and fucking you until you can't think of anything else but me. I think we've ignored our attraction to each other for far too long."

Hope gaped at him, stunned. "I'm leaving, and I'm not having sex with you." She fumed. "I'm…engaged."

"Another thing we need to talk about. Soon," Jason said ominously.

"There's nothing to talk about," she replied defensively.

I have to get away from him. Now.

He clasped both of her shoulders. "Exactly how much of our time in Vegas do you actually remember?"

What did that matter now? Obviously she'd gotten drunk enough to black out most of her return back to Colorado, and her recovery from her hangover from hell. "I remember seeing you. I remember going out for drinks. I don't remember much after that," she admitted, exasperated.

"Then you've forgotten a lot," Jason informed her ominously. "There will be no other men. You're not engaged to someone else. You're already married. To me," he finished fiercely. He took her left hand in his, entwined their fingers, and held the conjoined digits up to rest against his chest.

Hope gasped as her gaze landed on their entangled hands. The sparkle of the diamond on her finger twinkled mockingly back at her. Jason had a gold band on his left ring finger, and she sported an exquisite diamond ring that she'd been in too much of a fog to even notice earlier. "No." She shook her head adamantly in horror.

"Yes," Jason snapped back. "We're married, Hope."

"I can't be married to you. I couldn't have forgotten my own wedding." *Impossible!*

He let go of her hand and it fell back to her side. Wordlessly, he reached into his pocket and pulled out a piece of paper that he handed over to her.

Hope opened it frantically, looked at the marriage license as though it was a death sentence. She scanned the document and stopped at the signature at the bottom. It was shaky, but the signed name was hers, and she'd opted to use Jason's last name as her married name. "Oh, God. This can't be real." She groaned.

"It's very real. When I found it, I had the marriage checked out. It happened, Hope. The wedding is being recorded at the courthouse in Vegas," Jason replied coolly.

"We actually said vows?"

"Apparently, we did," he rumbled.

Hope's head reeled, her body nearly motionless with shock as she looked up at Jason's cold expression. His eyes bored into hers. "Were you drunk, too?" It had to be the only explanation. They'd both been out of their minds. "It's all just a big mistake. We can have it annulled. We can tell them neither one of us were of sound mind at the time," she told him breathlessly.

"I'd deny it," Jason answered ruthlessly. "Now that you're here, we have some unfinished business to resolve."

Hope broke her eyes away from Jason's and moved to the kitchen. She dropped the marriage license onto the counter and used the solid stone surface for support. She needed to figure this out, create some distance between her and Jason.

How in the hell did I let myself become Hope Sutherland, no matter how much I'd had to drink?

"Why would you deny it?" She looked at his face again from across the room. "This is a huge no-brainer, something that happened by mistake. We need to fix it."

He moved toward her with a savage grace that reminded her of a stalking, golden-haired lion. He placed a hand on each side of the cupboard, and effectively trapped her with his strong, muscular arms. "You know I want to fuck you, Hope. I think I made that abundantly clear last time we were together. But most of all, I don't want you marrying a man who will make you miserable. We can fuck each other until we're both satisfied, and then and only then, we'll get this marriage annulled."

"All of this, staying in a joke of a marriage, for just a screw?" Hope looked up at him, baffled and hurt by his atypical behavior. She couldn't see anything in his eyes except calculated determination, and it infuriated her as much as it made heat spiral in her core. This wasn't the Jason she knew. It was an entirely different part of him with which she'd never become acquainted. *Nice to meet you, jackass. Now where did you put the real Jason Sutherland?* "You can't make me stay with you."

"You think not?" he queried unemotionally. "What if I just tell your brothers that you've been lying to all of us for a very long time? How do you think they'll feel about that?"

Jason knew. "You wouldn't. They'd be hurt," Hope exclaimed desperately. She wondered just how much he'd discovered. Obviously, he'd found out about her career, her portfolio more than telling. *Dammit!*

"Then why did you do it, Hope? Why? How do you think your family would feel if something had happened to you and they never even knew about your career? What if you just disappeared in some natural disaster and they never knew what happened to you? It would kill all of them," Jason answered. Anger vibrated in his voice. "I know it sure as hell would have haunted me for the rest of my damn life."

"I don't understand why it would have bothered you at all. Why is this *any* of your business? We aren't friends anymore. We had an...encounter at the holidays, but that's all it was. I grew up a long time ago. I don't need your protection," she huffed, pushing furiously against his rock-solid chest. Apparently, he was angry, but she didn't appreciate his attempts at blackmail.

However, she couldn't let him tell her brothers. They'd be devastated that she hadn't shared her real life with them, but it was impossible for her to do that. They would tie her down, follow her constantly if they knew she was in danger, put her safety ahead of her anger at them. She couldn't do her job that way. Unfortunately, they'd also discover that she'd lied to them, and she loved her brothers more than anything. Lying to them had put a distance between her and her siblings that made her heart ache. But she hadn't seen any other way. After her stifling childhood, she'd needed to be free to pursue her own career, just like Dante had done when he'd become a homicide detective. However, being the youngest and only female in the family, her siblings did the overprotective older brother routine to perfection. They all had the money to have her watched constantly, and she'd never be able to bear that.

"I'm making it my business, Peaches," he told her gutturally. His hands came up to frame her face as his mouth descended on hers.

Peaches? He hadn't called her that since she was a child, when he told her that the reddish orange highlights in her hair reminded him of ripe peaches. She hadn't minded so much when she was younger and she'd needed a boost to her ego. He'd told her that ripe peaches were a good thing, and that her hair was unique. Now, the childhood nickname was a mockery coming from his mouth rather than the comforting epithet it had been to her when she was a girl.

"Don't call me that—" Her words were cut off as his mouth claimed hers in a demanding, furious embrace that almost immediately made her capitulate. She breathed in the now familiar, masculine scent of him. He tasted like mint, rich coffee, and pure carnal lust. His tongue speared through her lips, commanded her compliance.

Don't give in. He's being a bully. Don't give in.

Her treacherous nipples hardened against his chest, her longing suddenly stronger than her will to resist. She speared her hands into his *fuck-me-now* hair, fisted it and pulled his mouth harder against hers. Their mouths fused together, he ravaged her with every thrust of tongue. He pushed; she pushed right back.

Hope's yearning grew, and she moaned into his mouth, wanting so much more than she could possibly get. She'd wanted *him*, wanted *this* for so very long. But she wasn't able to give Jason what he wanted, even if she let him be a domineering bully, which she refused to do. Still, her body wanted, but what it really needed was a frustrating impossibility.

They broke the kiss, both of them breathing heavily. "Let go, Jason," she told him firmly and pushed against his shoulders. "Let go."

She wriggled out of his embrace as she swore she heard him whisper the word "never" softly. "I'm taking a shower and then I'm leaving."

"Take a shower," he rumbled. "And then we'll eat and you'll explain exactly why you felt it necessary to lie to everyone who cares about you. My threat wasn't idle, Hope," he warned her ominously.

"I'll always hate you for this," she told him angrily, furious with herself for still being so uncontrollably attracted to him when he acted like such a jerk. "What the hell is wrong with you? What happened to the Jason who actually rescued me from bullies instead of being one himself?"

"He grew up to be an asshole," he answered morosely, his azure eyes glacial and dark. "Hate me if it makes you feel better, but I'm not letting you leave here until I get what I want."

Bastard!

Hating Jason was easier with every word he uttered, and she strode over to him and let her hand fly, no thought in her head except to wipe the smug look off his face.

Smack!

The satisfaction of her hand as it connected with his frosty expression was more satisfying than the pain of her stinging palm. How dare he extort her just to get into her panties?

The shocked expression on his face was priceless, and Hope's anger continued to swell as he grasped her wrist to keep her from slapping him again.

Truthfully, not only was she pissed, but she was disheartened and wondered what had happened to the Jason she actually liked. This man was someone entirely different, and her heart mourned the loss of the man who had always kept her secrets without requiring anything in return.

"I guess this means you've decided to despise me?" He held his hand up to his reddened cheek. "But it doesn't matter."

For a brief moment, Hope thought she spotted an injured, sad look in his otherwise cold eyes...but in an instant, it was gone.

"I'm not sure how you expect me to feel any other way." Hope jerked her wrist from his grasp. "I admit...I got plastered, which I normally don't do. I admit...I haven't been exactly forthcoming about my chosen career. But that's my business. I'm a grown adult. What I do and don't choose to tell people is none of your business. I'm nothing to you, and you're nothing but an old childhood friend to me." *Liar!* Hope's racing heart was filled with sorrow and ached for the man she had so desperately wanted , one who was so different from the Jason she saw right now.

"You're far from nothing to me. And you can deny it all you want, but your body wants me even if you loathe me," he told her evenly. "You're married to me. Evidently, I didn't force you into wedded bliss. I have a ring on my finger, too, and nobody coerces me into anything. All I'm asking for is some time."

"You're asking me to be your whore to keep you from blabbing the truth to my brothers. You aren't asking for time, Jason. You're asking for a blackmailed prostitute," she answered furiously, breathlessly.

"I'm asking for time. The sex is just a given. Jesus, can't you feel the sexual tension between us?" He ran a frustrated hand through his hair. "And. You. Are. Not. My. Whore." His voice was full of wrath as he succinctly said each word with emphasis. "You're my wife."

"Not for long," she vowed, still upset, but also confused. Jason looked affronted by her description of his arrangement, and that didn't make sense. Wasn't it exactly what he was asking for? "And the sex is not a given. It's impossible."

Unable to hear another word without her heart being ripped from her chest, she left, almost running toward the bedroom. She locked the door and dragged clothes from her suitcase, surprised to find more jeans, shorts and other casual wear in a large bag beside her suitcase, things that had been at her condo. Someone had to have been in her home, which gave her the creeps. Whoever had brought Daisy here had also brought her more clothes. Hope shuddered with indignation. She snatched up a clean pair of jeans and a tank top, went into the bathroom and closed the door quickly, and locked it before the tears fell.

Jason picked up the keys to his rented vehicle, his heart heavy. So, Hope was going to end up hating him. Well, that would make two people in this house who hated him, because he detested himself right now, too.

Granted, he hadn't *exactly* lied. He'd just let her think he hadn't been coherent when they'd married, agreeing with her assumptions. Hell, she'd been pissed off enough because he forced her to stay. He could only imagine her fury when she discovered that he'd not only been totally sober, but that he'd orchestrated the whole thing from the beginning, made the marriage happen.

Jason had needed to remind himself that she'd lied, that she wasn't the woman he thought she was. That, and the fact that if he didn't do something now, she'd be miserable with a loser for the rest of her life, had made him capable of being a heartless bastard.

Yet, through the anger, Jason could see her disappointment, and it killed him.

His hand went to his still stinging, reddened cheek, and he smiled. The pain reminded him Hope could hold her own when she was furious. He could handle that. It was far better than the disillusioned look he'd seen her shoot at him, an expression that said she no longer trusted him.

Jason tried not to let that look haunt him as he walked out the door and locked it behind him.

Chapter 3

I can't hide in the bathroom forever.

Feeling much improved after her shower, Hope didn't even bother with makeup or drying her hair. She still felt lethargic from her hangover, and she wasn't looking forward to facing Jason again right now.

I need to find a way to keep him from talking to my brothers. There was a time when he could keep a secret. Can he do it now?

It rankled to give in to his demands, but she already knew she wouldn't have sex with him. Could she still trust him if she gave him the time and he didn't get what he wanted? Did she have enough faith to believe he wouldn't out her to her brothers or anyone else? The problem was, this was a different Jason from the young man she'd known as a child, and he wasn't even similar to the man who had rocked her world months ago with intimacies that she now craved.

So who the hell is the real Jason Sutherland? And how did I end up married to him?

How had she ever let that happen? *Stupid, stupid woman. What was I thinking?* Problem was, she obviously hadn't been thinking at all. She'd been severely impaired by way too much alcohol. The accidental meeting in Las Vegas with Jason had thrown her off balance.

She didn't remember much after he'd taken her into the hotel bar for a drink, but she remembered her fear that he'd discover her secrets. That's why she'd had one more drink—way too many times—to relax.

Somehow, it was hard to picture Jason getting so plastered that he'd married her, but he obviously had. He was a man who liked control, and it was difficult to imagine him giving that up and ending up married to her.

She stared at the glittering diamond on her left hand. The large stone winked back at her mockingly. It was beautiful in its simplicity, a single diamond set in a band engraved with delicate Celtic knots, yet she knew the large stone and intricate design had been expensive. "I have to end this," she whispered to herself fiercely. Her hand lowered to her side. It didn't really matter *how* this marriage had happened. What mattered was how fast she could get it dissolved and get Jason to not reveal her lies to her brothers. She needed to get back to the business of running her own life, even if Jason didn't approve.

Why did Jason even care? Obviously, he wanted to sleep with her, but what guy—what billionaire who could have any woman he wanted—married a woman like her, even if his brain *had* been temporarily incapacitated? Honestly, she couldn't begin to understand why he was threatening her just to spend time with her. Jason could make almost any woman drop her panties instantly. Why would he want to keep dragging this mistake out further just in an attempt to have sex with her—which was pointless anyway. It wasn't going to happen.

Pushy, arrogant, know-it-all man!

Maybe he *was* hurt and angry because he'd found out she was a liar, even though she wasn't sure why. Her lies hadn't really affected his life at all, although he *was* friends with her brothers. Maybe he was ticked because she'd lied to them, and perhaps he was a little bit justified if he was defending friends. Honestly, she'd probably always known that one day her lies would come back to bite her in the ass. She just hadn't known it would happen exactly like this. There was nobody she wanted to be indebted to less than Jason.

He'll never understand.

It was even less likely that the inflexible male she'd just butted heads with a short while ago would comprehend exactly *why* she needed to do what she'd done. Sometimes she wasn't even sure she completely understood it herself.

"End this, Hope," she said adamantly. She opened the bedroom door and forced herself to stride back to the living room.

Jason was just coming through the door with an armful of white paper bags. "Dinner," he remarked casually. "I don't cook well."

Hope took a few of the bags and set them on the kitchen table. "Hungry?" She looked at the enormous amount of food, momentarily forgetting her anger.

"Starving," he admitted with a sheepish grin. "I guess I over-ordered."

His smile put her off balance, the expression so much like the old Jason that her heart skipped a beat. She gnawed on her bottom lip in concentration as she tried to read him, to judge whether or not they could actually talk about this without getting angry.

At the enormous amount of food he'd purchased, she had to admit that he'd certainly had gotten carried away. Hope pulled plates out of the cupboard and unpacked huge burgers, fries, fried mushrooms, and even some Rocky Mountain oysters.

When they were both seated, they ate in silence; both of them concentrated on their food. Hope was famished now that her stomach had settled, and she didn't want to say anything to bring back the frosty Jason she'd battled with earlier. He seemed more relaxed, more approachable. She reached for a Rocky Mountain oyster and popped it into her mouth, and nearly moaned as she chewed. After a sip of her soda, she told Jason, "These are fantastic."

After he consumed the last of his second burger, Jason reached out and snatched one of the oysters. "The owner of the burger place told me they were a specialty of the restaurant." He ate one and reached for another. "These are good. I know they aren't really oysters. It tastes almost like chicken. What are they?" He put the second one in his mouth and gave her a questioning look.

Evilly, Hope waited until he was chewing before she answered. "Bull's balls. Calf testicles. They're actually really good when they're cooked properly. Nothing better than munching on some freshly fried balls," she told him teasingly as she took another oyster and popped it into her mouth and gave him an innocent look.

Score!

Hope bit back a smile as Jason nearly choked. He swiped up his soda and took several sips to wash down the oyster. His eyes narrowed in aversion. "That's disgusting," he grumbled. "Why didn't you warn me?"

She shrugged, unperturbed, but she'd been pretty certain he'd have this kind of reaction. Any one of her brothers would have reacted exactly the same way. "You're a well-traveled man. Don't you try out the local cuisine when you travel? Or are you just having sympathy pains for the bull?"

The disgruntled look on his face was priceless, and Hope itched to have her camera in her hands. Obviously, even if he was willing to eat just about anything, she guessed he drew the line at bull's balls. She'd lived in Colorado long enough to get used to crunching on the unusual Rocky Mountain specialty. She hadn't lied when she'd told him they were really good if they were cooked well, and the oysters he'd picked up were outrageously good…if you liked bull's balls.

"I've eaten all kinds of local cuisine, but there's something seriously wrong with eating—" He scowled at the oysters. "That."

Hope burst out laughing, nearly snorted as she saw a humorous side of Jason she'd never seen before. He looked like a little boy who didn't want to eat his peas, which really made her want her camera. She wasn't sure she'd ever see this look again, and she wanted to capture it. Smug, confident, panty-meltingly gorgeous Jason Sutherland actually looked like a rebellious child.

He pushed the remaining carton toward her. "It's not funny. Some things are just too personal to eat."

Hope chortled. "I'm sure they were personal to the bull, too. You *are* having sympathy pains. I take it you don't travel to Colorado very often."

J. A. Scott

"Rarely. And I've never been offered...those."

He couldn't even manage to say what they really were, which delighted Hope no end. "Why do I have a feeling that my brothers would feel the same way?" Hope smiled. Obviously testosterone-overloaded men had a real problem eating testicles.

"They would," Jason agreed with a grimace. "It makes me wish I could send some to Grady without him knowing exactly what they were."

"Admit it, if you didn't know what you were eating, you'd like them. They're pretty tasty." Hope cajoled him to confess that the local specialty was actually good. "They're even better if you have a tangy cocktail sauce, but they didn't give you any."

"But I *do* know what they are. And I can't believe you actually dip those in sauce." Jason gave her an unhappy look. "And you didn't warn me on purpose," he finished accusingly.

She *had* intentionally waited until he ate some of them, had wanted to see his reaction. It had pleased her more than she had expected. "Maybe I was trying to get back at you for threatening me, and for being such a jackass earlier. Staying married any longer than we have to is just compounding our stupid mistake."

His expression turned stormy. "You must have wanted the marriage, Hope. I'm sure I didn't force you."

Of course he hadn't. She'd obviously been all for the idea. There was no such thing as a shotgun wedding anymore, and she had to have been willing—probably because she had always wanted Jason so desperately. Her inhibitions had obviously all flown away and she'd readily agreed. "I wonder if I asked you." She wished she knew exactly what had happened.

"Maybe it was a mutual decision," Jason said casually as he got up and threw empty cartons away, grabbed a chocolate bar from the cupboard, tore off the wrapper, and consumed half of it in one bite.

It wasn't very romantic, but it was very possible she *had* asked *him*. Without her usual defenses, she might have even begged. Just the thought made her flush, her face now as red as her hair.

❧ 68 ❧

She tried not to think about their time in Vegas, so she rose and helped Jason clean up the table. "So how do you suppose we got the rings?"

"I imagine we purchased them like any other couple getting married," he said nonchalantly. His candy wrapper went in the trash since he'd already finished the entire bar of milk chocolate. "Do you like what we got?" His voice was casual, but she heard a note of indecision, a slight hesitation in his tone.

Hope sighed. "They're beautiful. But it's not like we're going to wear them." She twisted the ring she wasn't used to wearing on her finger, and started to draw it off.

"Leave it," Jason demanded as he turned around. "For now," he added in a low, husky voice.

Hope left it on her finger. What did it matter? She'd take it off eventually, though she found it odd that Jason still wore his, and he didn't want her to take hers off.

"What were we thinking?" She still fidgeted with the ring on her finger nervously. She wasn't given to mad acts of impulse, and she was certain Jason wasn't either. He was the type of man who weighed everything out, considered the pros and cons. He hadn't become a billionaire by not using his head.

He cornered her by the kitchen table, rested his hands on both sides of her and looked down at her with a set of turbulent blue eyes that made Hope shudder.

"I'm positive the head above my neck *wasn't* thinking. My dick was probably happily contemplating the consequences at the time, and in complete control." He leaned down until she could feel his heated breath against her lips. "Maybe I wasn't willing to see you married to anyone else but me."

He captured her mouth in a fierce embrace that made Hope's core clench in response. His kiss was possessive. Wild. All-consuming. It was the kind of embrace that she didn't have the strength to resist. Arms wrapped around his neck, she squeaked as his hands covetously palmed her ass and lifted her onto the table. His lips never left hers.

He tasted sinful, like the decadent chocolate he'd just consumed, and he was just as addictive. With a grasp on her hips, he yanked her heated core against his engorged cock none too gently and let her feel just how aroused she could make him.

For just a moment, Hope's heart beat erratically in satisfaction, and she immediately wrapped her legs around his waist, to feel him even tighter, closer.

Jason.

Her heart sighed and her body caught fire as Jason kissed her as if he had to have the connection, as if he needed her mouth more than he needed anything else.

Jason.

She tightened her legs around his waist, needed him so desperately that her core flooded with liquid heat. Her nipples hardened to sensitive twin peaks.

Jason.

She pulled her mouth from his, leaned her head back and moaned. Tears of frustration flowed down her cheeks.

I can't do this.

"Hope?" Jason put a hand behind her head and forced her to look at him. "What's wrong? Why are you crying?"

Hope looked into his passion-laden eyes, and felt helpless to explain. Gone was the jackass Jason, and the compassionate man she knew slowly returned. Unfortunately, his multiple personalities made everything more confusing. She wanted to confess everything to her old friend, the man who had given her such exquisite pleasure earlier in the year. The man who tried to extort her into staying with him—she wanted nothing to do with him. The problem was, deep inside, Hope knew that wasn't the real Jason. His cold ruthlessness might be a part of him, but it wasn't *all* that he was.

"Everything is wrong," she muttered. It felt as if the whole world suddenly crashed down around her. She pushed at his chest. "*This* is wrong. We should have never gotten married, Jason. I can't imagine either one of us behaving that way, but we did." This wasn't all Jason's fault. Certainly, he was playing a dirty hand right now, taking advantage of the situation, but she'd gotten drunk and apparently jumped on the chance to have a man she'd wanted for such an incredibly long time. Then, her lies had caught up to her with a vengeance. "I don't believe you did this for completely selfish reasons. Not if you were worried that I was marrying the wrong man at the time. Maybe some rational part of you was trying to save me."

Jason raised a brow. "Don't try to make me into a hero, Hope. I'm sure it was completely selfish. And my requirement for you to stay is definitely hedonistic."

"Then it was a waste of your time," Hope spat out at him. She stalked into the living room with Jason on her heels.

"I don't think you understand how badly I want you," Jason said ominously. He snaked an arm around her waist and pulled her down to the couch. "Let's hear about why you lied in the first place. Talk to me."

Hope landed on his lap, but she scrambled off him and seated herself on the other end of the sofa. She couldn't be close to him right now. She needed to out herself about some of her life and take her chances with Jason, even if she was still ticked about his highhanded tactics in trying to get her to stay. She swiped at the tears on her face. "You know about my photography career?"

"Obviously," Jason said acerbically. "It's hard to miss a portfolio full of pictures. It's also clear that you didn't want anybody to associate you with the billionaire Sinclair family, which is why you used your initials. What I don't understand is why you never told anyone."

Hope saw a flash of hurt in Jason's eyes. "Do you think my brothers would have been supportive?" She snorted. "I love them with all my heart, but they would have done everything they could to stop me from doing something I wanted to do. You know they would. For God's sake, they wanted me to have security even when I was in college. The only way I talked them out of that was by telling them that nobody associated me with the Boston Sinclairs, and I'd never tell anybody. After college, I had to let them think that I was living a very quiet, very anonymous life. Otherwise, they would have had security all over me, whether I wanted it or not. "

"Why does it have to be extreme weather?" Jason grumbled. He couldn't disagree with her point about her brothers.

Hope shrugged. "It started out as a fluke. I've always loved storms: the thunder, the lightning, and the unstoppable power of Mother Nature. Thunderstorms are brutally beautiful and fascinating because there's still so much we don't understand about extreme weather. Maybe it's the mystery that first intrigued me. I started right after school as a freelancer, most of my photos of lightning strikes and thunderstorms. Newspapers and other companies began to buy them, wanting more. I moved into it gradually, noticing that what I was photographing was what was most in demand. Eventually, I didn't wait for the storms to come to me. I went to them."

"So when most sane people were running away, you were running toward the storms?" Jason rumbled, still sounding upset.

Hope nodded. "Yes. I'm always as careful as I can be. Tornados are unpredictable, but David and I tried to be as cautious as we could be. Sometimes I wasn't so careful when I started. I was too naïve and intoxicated with being free to care. When you grow up beneath the iron fist of a raging alcoholic, and then are left to a mother who blames you because she can't move away somewhere else to forget the past, you learn to appreciate freedom. "

"Your mother blamed you?" Jason said angrily.

"Every single day. I was constantly reminded that if I didn't exist, she'd have her freedom. The day I graduated from high school was the happiest day of my life. I could finally stop feeling guilty for just existing." She cuddled Daisy on her lap as the feline leapt onto the couch.

Jason nodded his head toward her cat. "The same day that you got a deaf cat as a graduation present."

"I never regretted having her," Hope told him honestly. "She gives me unconditional love. She's been a great companion, Jason. She goes with me when I can take her, and she adapts to any environment, which is very strange for a cat." Hope wasn't about to tell him that she cherished Daisy just that much more because she'd gotten her from Jason.

"How did none of us ever figure this out for ourselves? Why did none of us know you were a photographer? How did your brothers never discover it?" Jason said, disgruntled.

"Because I didn't want anyone to know. I wanted my freedom. They believed I was living an idle, anonymous life in Aspen, traveling occasionally with friends. It's what I wanted them to believe."

"You know what you're doing is crazy, right? You're risking your life for pictures."

"It's my life to risk," Hope threw back at him. "And I don't think it's crazy. It's my job."

"I saw the pictures, Hope. The destruction and loss of life has to take its toll on you." He gave her a sharp glance.

That *was* the hardest part, the area of her job that ate at her soul. "It's horrible," she admitted. "I help when I can. I took first responder training. But yes, it's…difficult." She swallowed a lump in her throat at the truth. "Extreme weather is going to happen whether I'm there or not, and the victims are going to suffer horribly. I had to suck it up and try to help."

"What were you doing in Vegas? It's apparent to me now that you weren't there for a bachelorette party like you told me you were when we ran into each other. You would have been worried about contacting whoever you were with. There was nothing and nobody else in your room except your stuff." Jason looked at her, as though he mentally willed her to tell him the truth.

"I was there for a conference. I was asked to give a lecture on extreme photography. That's why I had my portfolio with me." Hope's stomach sunk as she revealed some more of her lies. "The party seemed like a good excuse when I slipped up and told Grady I was going to Vegas. I was tired that day. I'd just gotten back from Oklahoma. I was exhausted and I wasn't thinking clearly."

Jason raised his brows. "Ah, yes. The guy in some of your pictures. Where does he fit in?"

"David," she said in a choked voice. "He was an extreme meteorologist. We went to college together. He lived in Oklahoma, and we teamed up for tornado chasing. I learned a lot from him." Hope was breathless with disbelief that she was actually spilling all of this to Jason. But she could tell by the stubborn look on his face that he wouldn't stop until he got the truth.

"How good of a friend is he?" Jason asked hoarsely.

"He was probably my best friend." Hope watched Jason's face.

"Friends with benefits?" he asked gruffly.

Hope let out a startled gasp. Was he actually...jealous? "No. David wasn't into women that way."

"He's gay?" Jason looked relieved.

Hope nodded and teared up as she replied. "He was gay. He... died." She hated saying those words, hated to refer to David in the past tense. She still hadn't come to terms with the fact that her best friend, her only friend, was gone.

"When? How?" Jason asked in a gentle tone.

"Almost two weeks ago now. I was just coming back from his funeral and visiting with his family when Grady called me. I was close to his parents. I was physically and emotionally exhausted, Jason. I had no idea what I was saying to Grady. I was babbling."

"I'm sorry you lost your friend, Peaches," he utterly sincerely, tenderly. "What happened?"

Hope's heart still ached over losing David, but she answered shakily, "We don't know all the details. He was chasing a large tornado fairly close to his hometown. Witnesses say it suddenly changed direction, and it put David right in its path. I was here in Colorado because I was trying to get my lecture together for Vegas, so he was alone. He had nowhere to go, nowhere to hide. His truck was literally picked up and tossed down somewhere else. There wasn't much left of it." Tears streamed down her face. "I still can't believe he's gone."

"Jesus, Hope. You could have been in that truck." Jason's voice vibrated with fear. "I actually heard about the incident. I had no idea then that it was somebody you knew. It's one of the reasons I'm so freaked out about you chasing after tornados. People with decades of experience and a ton of knowledge can still die."

Hope nodded. She couldn't argue with him. Tornados were the most unpredictable of storms. Even with precautions, nothing was guaranteed because you could never completely predict its path. "I know. David was good, very cautious, and he still died. He was passionate about tornado research. He didn't do it for the adrenaline rush; he was trying to save lives, give people in the path of the tornado a longer warning." David had been one of the most compassionate men she'd ever known.

Jason moved over and pulled her onto her lap. His hands stroked over her back and her hair as she cried. "I know, sweetheart. I'm sorry. Please promise me you're done chasing tornados," he said gruffly as he buried his face in her hair. "Please."

The pleading note in his voice unraveled her. She sobbed and clung to Jason with her arms around his neck. "I can't do it anymore. Not without David. We were a team, and he was the one with all the knowledge. If I got any pictures I thought could be studied, I copied them and donated the photos for research."

"You're not doing it with anybody ever again. Promise me, Hope, before I lose my mind," he rasped against her neck. His body shuddered fiercely. "You could have been with him."

"I wasn't," she answered with a shaky voice. "And I promise." She couldn't bear to hear the fear in Jason's voice, and she never planned to chase another tornado. Losing David had torn her apart, and it was something she'd never do again without her friend.

"Thank Christ," Jason answered gutturally as he squeezed her body tightly.

"I miss him," she confided. "He knew me. He was the only one who really did." Her friend had known all of her secrets, but he was gone, and the emptiness in her soul was so profound that she had barely been able to function since his death.

"Let me know you again, Hope. Let me in. Please," Jason begged. His voice quavered with emotion.

"What if you don't like who I am now?" she asked hesitantly, so tempted to lean on Jason, let him take away some of her pain.

"I will. And I swear I'll never tell any of your secrets. Talk to me." He kissed her reverently on top of her head.

"We have to fix this marriage situation, Jason, before we can ever be real friends again," she told him softly.

"It will get fixed," he replied vaguely. "And I'm not sure we can ever be *just* friends again. I know I can't. I want to be your lover, too, Hope. I want you, and I know you want me, too."

"It's not that I don't want you physically," Hope said with a sigh. Why deny it? Why oppose him when he could feel her response every time he touched her? Her traitor of a body was a dead giveaway. "I just can't do it physically or emotionally."

"Your supposed fiancé? Bullshit. You don't love him and you know it. If you did, your body would never respond to me. I know you well enough to know that, Hope."

"It's not James. It's me. You understand now why I was out of my mind when I talked to Grady, and I wanted to get him to quit harping about me going to some billionaire fundraiser that you were attending in Colorado. He wanted me to go meet some decent guys. Like every billionaire is awesome?" She rolled her eyes. "Out of sheer frustration, I told him I was marrying James, and I'd be busy at the bachelorette party in Vegas. I shouldn't have said it, but I was willing to say just about anything to get him to leave me alone. I just wanted him to stop lecturing me and let me get off the phone."

"So your boyfriend didn't ask you to marry him?" Jason questioned warily.

"He didn't ask me anything at all. He doesn't exist. I made him up. I used my fictional boyfriend whenever I needed to get my brothers off my back or when I knew I was going to be out of touch for a while. James doesn't even exist."

Chapter 4

Hope knew she was doomed the moment that she saw Jason's incredulous expression. All of the energy he'd expended to blackmail her into staying here with him had been for nothing. She wasn't now—nor was she ever—going to marry. Maybe neither of them had known what they were doing when they got married, but Jason wasn't evil, and she had a feeling he wasn't trying to make her stay just because he wanted to get laid. Her upcoming marriage had to have had something to do with his drunken decision to marry her, and his subsequent refusal to let her leave. She had a hard time buying that he *just* wanted to screw her.

"You lied about him, too?" he growled. His eyes flashed like blue flames as he pulled back to look at her.

"Yes."

"Un-fucking-believable! Why the fake boyfriend?" He slid her off his lap and pinned her to the couch with his body. "Why the hell did you have to lie about that? Dammit! I want to know you again, Hope, but I don't fucking understand you."

Letting him know her was much too dangerous. Somehow, she needed to push him away, even though her heart didn't want to. "Same reason. My brothers were always trying to hook me up with anybody they knew when they were traveling to Colorado. I didn't want to be fixed up. Finally, I made somebody up. In spite of the fact that I do it a lot, I actually lie very badly. I stumbled when they asked his name, coming up with something completely unoriginal. I panicked when they wanted to know what he did, who he worked for. I knew they'd be spying. I had to make him unemployed."

"And the breakup before you went to Grady's for the holidays?"

"We had to break up because Grady wanted me to bring him along with me. What do you think he would have said if my unemployed fiancé couldn't make it to his engagement party?"

Jason's nearness made her body ache with unfulfilled desire, but her brain protested; his anger stifled her. "Please get off me, Jason," she pleaded. She needed distance.

"Christ!" he hissed vehemently. "Everything about you is a lie."

"Yes." She breathed heavily. She felt trapped by the angry man above her, even though she knew he'd never hurt her. "Everything."

I need to push him away. It's better if he hates me.

Hope struggled to get away from him. She needed air; she needed space. "So now you know. There was never any reason for you to marry me, and certainly no reason to try to make me stay." She pushed against his chest, his strong body as immovable as a stone wall.

"Oh, there is a reason I want you here now. I want to fuck you, Hope. For some reason I can't get you out of my system. I might not like you very much right now, and I sure as hell don't understand you, but I still want your body," Jason rasped, apparently not happy about that fact.

"Get. Off." Hope gasped now, desperate to get away. His angry voice, his large, unyielding form suffocated her.

"I plan to get off," he told her bitterly. "Inside you."

"No!" Hope clawed at him to get away, and she panted heavily. "I can't. Stop, Jason. Please." The words left her mouth as a desperate plea.

"Jesus." Jason sat up and his hand scraped through his hair savagely. "What the hell is wrong with you? One minute your body is responding to me like you want me as much as I want you. And then, a few seconds later, you're fighting to get away."

Hope sat up quickly and raked her hair out of her face with a trembling hand. "I don't want you. I just need to get out of here, annul this disastrous marriage and move on with my life. I don't want you to tell my brothers, but I can't stop you."

Jason's furious eyes bored into her. One of the muscles in his jaw twitched wildly.

Hope had never seen Jason this irate.

"You're staying for two weeks. When you leave, I'll never say a word to your brothers," he demanded, his expression cold and calculating.

"I can't. I'm busy right now," she tried to explain. Now that he knew her fiancé was a sham, why did he still want her to stay?

"I don't give a shit. The last thing you need is to be out chasing fucking storms, even if they aren't tornados. You're staying here. Take the deal or I'll tell every single one of your brothers and you'll have more people on your ass than the president of the United States."

Okay. Now he's trying to stop me from doing my job because it's dangerous. Even though I agreed not to chase tornados anymore, he doesn't want me to chase any storms at all.

Hope stood up, indignant and pissed off. Jason might not like how she ran her life, but he didn't have the right to interfere. "I can't do what I do without anonymity," she told him heatedly. "Even if I'm not chasing tornados, I still have a job to do. There's plenty of other extreme weather."

Jason rose and looked down at her. His towering strength was meant to intimidate her. "Then I guess that's a problem. You'll suddenly be famous. H.L. Sinclair, the known photographer, will become even more famous because she's part of the mega-wealthy Sinclair family. The media will be all over that."

Dammit! The press would be all over *her*, too. It would be the end of her career. She couldn't do what she did with a freaking entourage. Her fury with Jason exploded, and her hand flew toward his face in outrage.

He caught it before it connected with his cheek. "Don't try it again. No woman has ever succeeded before you, and it's not happening a second time." A firm, strong hand held her wrist next to his face.

"Bastard," she hissed. She hated him for what he was doing.

"You finally got that right." Jason's icy eyes ran over her face impassively. "Do we have a deal or not?"

Hope contemplated her alternatives, and came up with...nothing. "No sex." She yanked her wrist from his hand and lowered it back to her side. "I'll give you two weeks, but I'll make your life miserable while I'm doing it." He would be suffering the entire two weeks, and she could do it without even trying, just by being her own, broken self. Jason was about to find out that he couldn't have what he wanted from her. Fine. She'd give him his damn two weeks, and he'd be glad to get rid of her after those days had passed.

"There *will* be sex and plenty of it," Jason countered. "I'm not sure what game you're playing, but you want this as much as I do," he said in a sultry, low voice, but his expression was still cold. He lifted a lock of her hair and toyed with it. "Are you still a virgin, Hope?" His tone was gentler.

She snorted and batted his hand away. "Are you kidding? That was taken away from me years ago."

"Obviously somebody did a pretty poor job of it," he observed casually. "Stop fighting this, Hope. Stop fighting us. It's going to happen. And it won't be unwillingly. I'm not into taking women by force."

"If you want me, you'll have to," she retorted sharply.

"We'll see, Peaches. Two weeks is a long time. I expect you to do everything I want, short of fucking you. That will happen when you're ready to admit you want me as much as I want you."

Even infuriated, Hope was already ready to admit that, but it didn't matter. "I want your promise that you'll let me leave at the end of the two weeks, never expose me and never bother me again," she told him abruptly.

She saw him flinch briefly. A wounded look crossed his face before it was gone. It had only been an instant, but she'd hurt him, and her heart ached because of it. No matter how big of a jackass he was at the moment, this wasn't the Jason she'd grown up with. He couldn't have changed that much. Somewhere in that complex brain of his, he thought he was protecting her.

"Agreed," he said hoarsely.

"I'd like some time alone. I'm going to take a bath." She needed to relax, give her body and mind a chance to calm without Jason's presence. Her body still trembled with reaction, and she needed room to breathe.

"I have a better idea." He took her hand and pulled her firmly back down the hallway toward the bedroom.

Hope went, her body tense, but trusting Jason enough that she didn't think he was about to forcibly take her. They passed the master bedroom they'd slept in, continued to the end of the long hallway, and he pulled her into another guest room. She startled until he went to a sliding glass door and they exited the inside of the house and followed a rock pathway for a short distance before he stopped.

She recognized the rocky, steaming pool immediately. "Hot springs." She sighed. The smell of minerals and the warm, humid air instantly relaxed her. It was a good-sized pool in a natural setting, large boulders that could be used as seats beside the water, and a mini waterfall where a person could sit on several levels.

"You're familiar with them," Jason guessed. The anger left his voice.

"We have a large hot springs not far from Aspen. I knew Rocky Springs was one of the largest natural hot springs, but I've never been here." She looked longingly at the pool. "And I didn't know they had private pools here."

"I never got to try it last time I was here," Jason admitted huskily.

"You should," Hope confided. "It's amazing." It was starting to get dark, and the heat of the day in the mountains was over. It was a fantastic time to sink into the hot springs.

Jason unbuttoned his shirt. "Come with me," he cajoled quietly.

Hope's mouth went dry as he exposed his massive chest. "I don't have a swimsuit," she sputtered as she watched as though compelled while he revealed those perfectly formed abs and chest.

His blue eyes grew darker, more like sapphires, in the dim outside lighting, and they were persuasive and hot as they roamed her body. "It's private. Get naked. It isn't like I haven't seen you that way before," he reminded her smoothly.

Hope hesitated. Her eyes were glued to his nimble, strong fingers as he unbuttoned his jeans, a sexy happy trail revealed at an agonizingly slow speed. She held her breath, and waited. And waited. And waited. Finally, he slipped out of the jeans he wore, and took the boxer briefs with them. Hope nervously licked her suddenly dry lips as Jason stood in front of her, gloriously nude. Not that he needed to be shy. Jason was...absolutely perfect, from his *fuck-me* messy hair and fathomless blue eyes, to his sculpted, ripped body that was covered in golden skin.

Oh God, I want to touch him.

He moved to the pool, and gave Hope a glimpse of his firm, toned backside that made her want to grope it just to see if it was really as hard as it looked.

"Are you coming?" Jason asked with false innocence.

He was completely aware of how he affected her—smug bastard. She watched as he immersed himself immediately, no waiting like he should have done, and emerged from the water with his skin shimmering from the moisture and his hair plastered to his head.

Oh. My. God.

He moved to the side of the pool closest to her and rested his forearms on the rock surface. "I'm not going to force you into anything or attack you, Hope. Come relax with me."

He didn't smile, but his expression had softened. Hope was torn. She wanted to climb into the water, let the seductive warmth soothe her. She was lonely, still torn up over David's death, and she wanted company. Yet, she was still surprised by Jason's earlier cold, nasty demeanor. Yes, she'd lied, but not directly to him, and they didn't even really connect as friends anymore. Yes, they'd had that incredible

New Year's rendezvous. Still, his reaction had been pretty extreme considering the fact that they'd been distant before and after that night.

Maybe both of them were screwed up, neither one knowing the other anymore. Jason was uncovering all of her emotions, things she buried so deeply inside her that she didn't think they were ever going to surface. He could fire her temper faster than any man on earth, including her brothers. Lord knew he had definitely ignited a sexual spark, an intensity she'd never experienced before. He was tender when she needed comfort, made her want to lean on someone for the first time in her adult life. He could make her laugh one moment, and make her want to cry the next. That range of emotions was exhausting, and she wasn't sure where she wanted their relationship to go from here. Letting him touch her heart would be disastrous. He might want her for now, but she'd end up destroyed later.

Don't overthink it, Hope. Do what you want to do.

Hope wanted to stay, to sink into the warm water, and enjoy not being alone. Jason was right about one thing: he *had* seen her body before. Being shy around him now didn't make any sense. She tore her clothes off quickly anyway, to expose herself as little as possible. Her body flushed as she felt the heat of his eyes on her.

"Jump." He held his arms out to receive her body.

He doesn't realize what he's asking, how unlikely I am to ever trust someone to catch me.

"Where's your sense of adventure, Peaches?" he asked lazily.

He challenged her, and she knew it. Unfortunately, she had a really hard time ignoring provocation.

She jumped.

And Jason caught her easily and confidently.

With a firm grasp around her waist, he let her body slide slowly down the front of him, ever so slowly, until her feet finally hit the ground in chest-high, pleasantly hot water. She spun herself out of his arms and immersed herself in the pool. The stress of the day slowly seeped out of her body. "This is amazing." Her head popped back up and she swept the hair from her eyes.

"Maybe I should get one in my penthouse in New York City," Jason said teasingly.

"I think the best you're going to do is a Jacuzzi," Hope answered with a laugh. Her heart raced as she took in the small, devilish grin on his face. Moisture beaded on his chest and shoulders, and made her want to slowly lick off every drop. "I don't think you're going to find natural hot spring pools where you live unless you get out of the crowds, city boy."

"I already have a regular hot tub," Jason replied with a mockingly petulant look.

"Aw, poor little billionaire. Find something you actually can't have?" She scooped up a handful of water and splashed him with it.

The sun had set completely, and as Hope looked up, she could see the stars appear. Distracted, she never saw Jason coming. He wrapped a steely arm around her waist and pulled her under the water, and kept her imprisoned after she surfaced. Sputtering, she tried to retaliate, and hooked her ankle around his legs to try to take him down. Unfortunately, he was ready for it, and he barely moved. With a booming, low laugh, he picked her up and sat them both down on one of the wide, rock ledges; he pulled her between his legs, her back to his front, and wrapped his arms around her waist. "When are you going to learn not to start something you can't finish, Peaches?" he asked in a husky baritone.

Feeling lethargic from the water, and tired of fighting, she leaned her head back against his shoulder. She could feel the probing heat of his erection against the small of her back, but it wasn't disconcerting. His body was relaxed, his head resting against the natural headrest on the stone pool.

"Tell me where you've been, Hope, what you've been doing." He sounded resigned and curious.

The water lapped against her chest. "I've been just about everywhere. India, Japan, the Philippines, Mexico, Hawaii…anywhere that there's been extreme weather or natural events, I've been there. During the spring and summer, David and I teamed up and tracked super cells, mostly around Tornado Alley. This time of year, I'm mostly getting ready to start tracking hurricanes here in the US and I was chasing storms with David." Her voice cracked with despair, and Jason's arms tightened around her protectively, reflexively, in silent comfort.

"When are you home?"

"Almost never," she admitted. "Mostly in the winter."

"For the avalanches and blizzards?" Jason asked ironically.

"Mostly for the skiing," she answered cheekily. "And the Bronco games."

"Seriously?" Jason sounded falsely outraged. "You switched your loyalties to the Broncos? What happened to the Patriots? You're a Boston girl."

"I'm fickle," she answered teasingly. "The Broncos stole my heart."

"They haven't won a Super Bowl in fifteen years," Jason grumbled into her ear.

"Broncos fans are loyal. They'll win eventually. There's always this year."

"I can't believe I'm married to a woman who isn't a Patriots fan," he replied unhappily as he toyed with the ring on her left finger.

Married.

For a brief period of time, she'd forgotten, completely relaxed in Jason's arms. "Good thing it's not permanent," she replied lightly. "I don't think I could be married to a Patriots fan either."

He was silent for a moment. "Do I want to know how close you were to some of those tornados? Do I want to know about every close call you've had? I've seen the pictures, Hope, and I already know how close you came to dying with your friend. I'm so fucking grateful that you had to plan for Vegas." His voice wavered as he mentioned her close call. "You're incredibly talented, but I want you to reconsider what you're doing."

"I do have telephoto lenses. I can bring the images far closer than they really are." She smiled weakly, her body limp from the warm water. Even though it wasn't exactly a compliment, it felt good to hear Jason say she had talent. She'd never really needed validation, but it was nice to have someone she knew, someone who was close to her brothers, know about her career. The only person in her life who'd supported her was David.

"But you know the dangers," he rumbled.

"David's death hit close to home for me. I do know, and I'm not chasing tornados anymore, Jason."

"And what about the hurricanes, cyclones, and typhoons?"

"I'm as careful as possible. I try to stay on high ground because of the storm surges, and I base myself in a building that should be able to withstand the wind speeds," she told him carefully.

"Should be?" he grunted.

Hope shrugged. "Nothing in life is guaranteed, Jason. Anything we do has risks. Just getting into a vehicle every day is risky. But we do it."

"The vehicle is usually moving away from danger, not toward it." His voice was graveled and raspy.

"Can we just call a truce? Just for tonight? Tell me what you've been doing since you finished school…other than making a ton of money and becoming one of the hottest bachelors in the world." She wanted to know what Jason's life had been like, where he'd traveled. She also wanted to know whether there had been any important women in his life, even if it was none of her business. They were separating soon, but she was still curious. "How's your mom?" Hope had always liked Jason's mother.

"She's good. It took her a long time to get over my dad's death, but she's doing well now," Jason answered warmly, the affection he had for his mother clearly evident.

"I never got to tell you that I was sorry about your dad. He was a good man." Jason had lost his father just as he graduated from college, and she hadn't seen him during that year because she was in her first year at the university. Unfortunately, she hadn't even heard about his father's death until the funeral was over; Grady informed her during one of their routine phone calls.

"He was a very good man," Jason agreed. "But he wasn't a great businessman. When I took over his company, it was nearly broke."

"How?" she asked in a shocked voice. Jason's family had lived close to hers, right down the street in a mansion just as big as their own. His dad had been as wealthy as her father. "He was rich."

"He wasn't," Jason confessed roughly. "He was trying to keep up the façade, but he had some bad investments, sunk a lot of money into companies that didn't fly."

"Oh, God. I'm sorry. I didn't know. Did my brothers know?" Hope knew any one of her brothers would have stepped in and helped Jason out.

"Nobody knew. You're the only person I've ever told other than the upper management of his company. Even my mother never knew. I couldn't bring myself to let her know that my dad didn't leave her with much," he confessed reluctantly. "I just tried to pick up the pieces after he died. I did some risky things, took some calculated bets that paid off. Then I did it again and again."

Hope was willing to bet that they weren't all that risky. Jason was brilliant, had a sharp mind for investing. If he thought a company would fly, he had reason to believe it. "So you rebuilt the company and became wealthy all over again. By yourself."

"I got lucky in a few areas, but yeah. Then I started my own investing. I found out I was damn good at making *some* money into *more* money. A lot more money."

"Have you ever had a bad investment?" Hope was now awed by what Jason had accomplished. She'd thought he was a rich boy who'd gone on to become a richer man.

Jason shrugged. "Rarely," he said without any false arrogance. "If I do, I cut my losses quickly and move on. That's one thing my father didn't do and it nearly ruined him."

"How do you know if an investment is good?"

"It's mostly analysis," Jason answered nonchalantly.

It was more than that, and Hope knew it. If it could be done strictly by analysis, a hell of a lot more people would be rich. Jason had a gift for sniffing out good investments, an excellent gut instinct combined with that analysis. "You have a talent, Jason. I think you're incredible. What you've accomplished is almost impossible, yet you did it."

He was silent for a moment, almost as if he didn't know how to answer. After a few minutes, he rose and took her with him.

"I think we're both waterlogged," he grunted. He placed her gently on the side of the pool so she could get out, and hefted himself out behind her.

"I need a shower," she muttered. "If I don't, the minerals irritate my skin." She stood and quickly opened the doors of a mini closet next to the pool. One towel she tossed to Jason; the other she used to quickly dry her hair. She wrapped the fluffy material around her body, and then snatched a bottle of water from one of the shelves. After she drank half of it, she passed it to him. "It's not cold, but it's hydration."

Jason chugged the rest of the bottle quickly and tossed it into the nearby trash. He ran the towel over his body roughly and then wrapped it around his waist.

"A shower sounds good," Jason said abruptly. He grabbed her hand and hauled her toward the door. "Let's go."

Hope nearly lost her towel as she was hurtled forward to follow in Jason's wake.

Chapter 5

J ason had always considered himself a thinker, a man who calmly considered his options before he made a decision. Rarely was he short-tempered or was his mind muddled. However, Hope Sinclair—Hope Sutherland, that was—slowly and thoroughly made him completely lose his head.

Slowly, his perception of her morphed in his mind, but his dick felt the exact same way about her as it always had: beyond ready, completely willing, and so damn able to be inside her that he was ready to snap.

He had so many reasons to be angry with her now:

She'd lied to everybody—check!

She was a completely different person than he'd thought she was—check!

She was independent and stubborn—check, and check!

The problem was, she was still Hope: still the funny, sweet, and bighearted woman she'd always been. She was also talented and ballsy, which he admired. Honestly, he had to admit that if he only passively looked at the situation, he could probably understand why she'd wanted to pursue her career anonymously and not tell her brothers. She was right. They would have wanted to protect her, and they definitely would have made pursuing her career difficult for her because of those protective instincts. The problem was, he didn't look at the whole situation indifferently, and he wanted to physically restrain her from ever doing anything risky ever again.

In addition, her mind-boggling Jekyll-and-Hyde attitude about sex drove him completely insane.

She wanted him.

She responded to him.

She looked at him with fire and heat in her eyes.

He could bring her to an incredible climax with his mouth.

Still, he couldn't fuck her. *What. The. Hell?* Something was happening with Hope, and for the life of him, he couldn't figure out exactly what it was that stopped her from letting go of her inhibitions. She wasn't a virgin, so her hesitation wasn't caused by a lack of experience.

It was going to be up to him to show her how incredible it could be between the two of them. Hopefully soon, before his dick shattered from constantly being as hard as a rock.

Worse, he could feel her tension, her needs, and it made him almost frenzied to make her come, hear her moan his name when she did.

Jason wanted to turn the shower on full blast to the cold setting, but he didn't because he was dragging Hope into the shower with him. He dropped his towel and divested her of hers before he stepped into the warm water and pulled her in behind him.

Jesus. If he didn't touch her soon, he would lose it. He watched as she reached for the liquid soap and lathered her body. Taking the bottle from her, he squeezed a generous amount into his hands and helped her.

"Jason," she said tremulously. Her eyes opened to give him a startled look as his fingers glided over her breasts.

"I'm not screwing you, Hope. I'm just taking care of you," he rasped. "Let me."

She released a small whimper as he moved her hands to her side and pulled her back against his front. He now had full access to her beautiful breasts. He cupped them, circled his thumbs around her nipples, and was gratified when they hardened beneath his fingers. His strokes and teasing brought them to sensitive peaks before he pinched them lightly between his fingers.

"Jason." Hope moaned and leaned her head back against his shoulder.

Was there anything better than hearing her moan his name? Maybe being inside her while she screamed his name in climax, but he was content for the moment.

Her body slick with soap, Jason's hand glided down her abdomen smoothly, before he parted the slit in her flesh between her thighs to seek and then find her clit. She moaned the second he brushed his finger along the sensitized bundle of nerves. Her body shuddered as he used her own moist heat to drench his fingers and allowed them to easily slide over her clit. "You're so wet, so hot," he said harshly in her ear. He breathed heavily as he realized that she was so ready for *him*.

"I need—" Her voice broke off in a tortured groan.

At that moment, Jason needed nothing else but to satisfy her. She wanted. She needed. He'd be the man to deliver for her.

One of his hands worked her nipples as his fingers increased the strength and speed of his strokes on her clit. Her body shook. "Come for me, Hope."

"I don't think I can stop it," she cried desperately.

"No stopping. Let go." Jason tormented her body without mercy. He was ready to feel her come apart for him.

"Yes. Oh, God. Jason." She panted; her body shook more, and she splintered in his arms.

Mine. She's mine.

As she climaxed, Jason's possessive instincts took hold, and he moved his hand from her breast and thrust two fingers into her channel, felt her muscles spasm and clench against them as she found her release. As he found his reward, her flesh tightened around his fingers and clutched at the digits as she came.

Her horrified scream brought him back to reality.

"No! Stop! No!" Hope thrashed against him, trying desperately to escape.

Jason tore his hands away and turned her body until he could hold her against his chest. "Hope. Stop. It's okay, sweetheart. What happened?"

His heart pounded violently against his chest wall, and he clutched her body against his with a strong grip, unable to let her go.

What the hell was happening? It was almost as if she were possessed: her nails clawed at his chest, and her screams echoed through the bathroom, a bloodcurdling howl of pain and terror that he knew he'd never forget. "Hope," he bellowed over her screams. "Talk to me."

She calmed slowly, as though she were coming out of a daze. "Jason?" she sobbed.

"It's me, baby. It's me."

"Oh, God. I'm so sorry." She put her face against his chest and wept.

He held her just like that, losing track of time. His hand ran over her wet hair and back until she stopped sobbing. Jamming a hand against the shower controls, he stopped the water and stepped out of the cubicle. She stood in the shower, not saying a word, as he dried her off with a towel. He ran the towel briefly over his own wet skin before he discarded it. Then, he picked her up and carried her to bed.

She shivered as he climbed in beside her, and he quickly brought her against him. "Do you want me to turn on the light?" he asked hoarsely, not sure what else he could do to help her. The room was dark, the shutters closed; only the light from the hallway gave the bedroom a very dim illumination.

"No." She threw her leg over his and almost climbed on top of his body. "Don't leave me, Jason."

He released a tense breath and tightened his hold on her. "I'm not going anywhere. I promise."

Jason's decision was made right then and there: he would never go anywhere if Hope needed him.

Protective instincts had flared the moment he'd heard her scream, nearly giving him heart failure. He didn't know what had happened, but he'd figure it out. Right now, all that mattered was the woman in his arms. He needed her to feel safe again.

He was awake a long time after she had fallen asleep, trying to will whatever demons that plagued her to go back to Hell. Eventually, after he was sure she slumbered peacefully in the shelter of his arms, Jason slept.

Hope woke early the next morning. Her limbs were still entwined with Jason's, his arms holding her as if he protected her.

She slipped quietly out of the bed and got dressed in a pair of denim shorts and a forest green short-sleeved shirt. After brushing through the messy hair she hadn't brushed out the night before, she scrounged through her makeup case until she found a clip to confine the wayward strands. She snatched her sneakers, her trusty Nikon and the case, and then snuck out of the bedroom just as the sun began to rise.

Jason stayed peacefully asleep—thank God!—so she didn't have to do an early morning confrontation. Last night had been humiliating, and she wasn't sure how to explain herself to him. She'd thought she was over extreme reactions, finally done with the terror that had eaten her alive from the incident that had occurred over three years ago.

I haven't tried to have sex except for that night with Jason.

She hadn't, and maybe she shouldn't be experimenting now. Jason could make her body fly apart...but only up to a certain point. After finally finding some peace, she wasn't certain she should do anything to relive the experience that had shattered her life.

She put on her tennis shoes—minus socks because she wasn't going into the bedroom again to search for a pair—and went into the kitchen.

Make coffee or not?

She was useless without caffeine, but she didn't want to linger, so she pulled a can of sugary soda loaded with caffeine from the fridge and, with a smile, grabbed one of the candy bars on the counter.

He's still a chocolate addict.

She'd rarely seen Jason without something chocolate-covered in his hand when he was younger, and his habits obviously hadn't changed. For some reason, she found that comforting. She smiled as she wondered whether he'd notice she'd snatched one of his Snickers bars. He'd always shared with her when he was younger, but he was pretty possessive about his chocolate.

The door opened quietly, so she slipped outside and closed it softly behind her. With her camera pulled from its case, she slipped the strap around her neck and quickly adjusted the lens to have it ready in case she ran across any wildlife. As she surveyed the area, she decided to follow what looked like a well-traveled path through the woods, and opened the soda and candy bar as she walked. The strap of the camera case was slung cross-body style to get it out of the way, and she kept walking so her legs didn't have a chance to get cold. It had cooled off considerably during the night, as it always did at high altitude, but it would warm up as soon as the sun got higher and brighter.

It didn't take her long to finish the chocolate bar, and she swigged on her soda, waking up as she felt the sugar and caffeine kick in.

Hope stopped occasionally to get shots of the mountains. The narrow path opened up into a grassy field. She froze as she saw the creek that ran down the middle; the most enormous bull moose she'd ever seen fed lazily along the water. Moving slowly, she watched for any signs of aggression as she shot pictures of the majestic animal with grizzled brown fur and the biggest rack of horns she'd ever seen. She knew the moose had spotted her, but the large mammal ignored her. Its only natural predator was the wolf, so the moose didn't look too concerned about her, but she kept her distance, lined up shot after shot of the incredible creature as she adjusted her lens and the camera to get different angles.

Her landscape photos and wildlife pictures had grown in demand, even though she was known for shooting extreme weather. As she took each photo with a relaxed sense of awe, Hope enjoyed every moment she spent with the glorious creature before it wandered away, back into the woods.

"You'll see elk and bear here sometimes, too." A deep voice commented behind her. "It's a popular watering hole for wildlife."

Hope whirled around. Her heart nearly thumped out of her chest as she faced the voice, a man who was only a few feet away from her. With a hand to her chest, she told him breathlessly, "You scared me."

"Sorry. I didn't want to scare the moose away," he answered, his hands in the pockets of his jeans.

Hope gaped at him. The man was around Jason's age, with gorgeous blond hair cut short and neat. He was dressed casual in jeans and a long-sleeved pullover, his feet in a very nice pair of hiking boots. He looked at the ground, but when his head rose to glance at her, Hope froze in utter shock. She recognized that face, that pair of smoky gray eyes framed by thick, gorgeous eyelashes. "C-Colt?"

"Hello, H.L. Sinclair," he responded with a weak grin. "We meet again."

Hope was speechless, astonished to see the man who she'd only met briefly, yet had played such an important role in her life. She couldn't quite believe he actually stood in front of her. She closed her eyes and opened them again, but Colt still stood right in front of her.

"How are you?" His expression grew shadowed.

"I'm good. I can't believe you're here," she answered slowly.

"My real name is Tate Colter. I sort of belong here," he answered teasingly.

"You're Tate Colter?"

"Last time I checked," he shot back jokingly. He held out his arms to her as he coaxed her with another small grin that uncovered an attractive dimple in his cheek. "Hug me. You know you want to."

"Oh. God." Hope sprang at him and threw herself into his outstretched arms. "I never got to say thank you. I never saw you again." Tears rolled down her cheeks as she hugged the man who had saved her life with a death grip around his neck. "Thank you, Colt. Thank you for everything you did for me."

He hugged her back and rocked her body slightly. "I was just doing my job, Hope. I wasn't even sure you'd recognize me. You certainly didn't a few days ago."

How could she not recognize Colt? He'd been her savior, and those beautiful gray eyes had been unforgettable. "I was really drunk when we came in," she admitted. "Did I meet you here?" she asked, confused.

"I flew you and Jason back here to Rocky Springs. I was with him in Vegas. You passed out before we landed, and we didn't see each other until you were completely wasted."

"Not one of my finer moments," she answered, disgruntled. She pulled back to look at him. "I'm so happy to see you."

"Most women are," he told her mischievously.

Hope smiled back at him. She couldn't help it. Colt—or was it Tate?—had been cocky as hell, but she'd needed that confident assurance three years ago, had hung onto it with everything she had back then. "Tell me how a billionaire Colter ended up in Special Forces," she requested curiously.

"I'm a rebel," he answered nonchalantly. "It probably happened much the same way as a wealthy Sinclair became an extreme weather photographer," he teased. "My cabin is just over this hill. Want some coffee?"

"Definitely," she agreed gratefully and followed him as he let her go and led the way. A comfortable silence settled between them for a while, before Tate spoke. "I guess I'm as curious as you are," Tate mused. "I'm wondering how a very wealthy Sinclair ends up traveling alone in a foreign country without protection. I never connected you with *the* Sinclairs. It's a fairly common last name. And I never knew your first name."

"I didn't want anyone to know." She picked her way along a path that led uphill.

"Does Jason know what happened?" Tate asked solemnly. "I recognized you when I saw you in Vegas, but I never said a word."

She stared at his wide back in front of her. "Thank you for not saying anything."

At the top of the hill, he turned around and took her hand to help her up a short, rocky incline. "I hacked into your computer when we got back to Rocky Springs," he confessed, totally remorseless.

"Why?" She looked at him quizzically as she stepped up beside him.

"Because I could," he said devilishly. "You need to buy better computer protection. I wanted to see what you'd been up to in case you didn't recognize me. You went back to chasing storms."

She knew she should be angry because Colt had broken into her computer, but she couldn't muster any anger. Hope nodded slowly. "I had to go back."

Tate nodded. "I understand. But I think you need to tell Jason. He was totally clueless, Hope. The guy married you. He cares enough to know. I only outed you about your career. He was going to find out anyway. But it's not my place to tell him anything else, or even that we've met before. It's your story to tell."

She followed as he strode toward a large home at the top of the hill. "He was drunk when he married me, and he just wants to get into my panties," she told Colt, appalled as soon as the words came out of her mouth. She barely knew Colt, even though he'd been an important person in her life for a very brief time.

Tate chuckled. "Here's a newsflash for you, Hope: that's what most men want. And they don't need to marry a woman to get it. That's not all that Sutherland wants."

"Colt, he said—"

"He's full of shit," Tate said confidently. "And call me Tate. Colt was just my code name."

Hope stopped short as she got a good look at the home Tate was headed for. "*This* is your *cabin*?"

He shrugged. "It *is* made out of logs."

Hope gaped, trying to take in the sheer size and design of Tate's house. It was made of cedar logs and stone, with large pillars of cedar across the front of the home. Towering picture windows adorned the front of the house, probably giving an incredible view of the sunsets. It was at least two stories, probably three as she was fairly certain one of the sets of stairs led to a lower level. There was a garage connected with several doors, a section of the home that could probably store half a dozen vehicles. Strangely, the home was designed to fit into the wooded mountain setting, and even though it was enormous, it still managed to be welcoming rather than ostentatious. "It's beautiful," Hope said breathlessly. "Can I take pictures?"

Tate waved his hand, and taking that as permission, Hope took several shots before she followed him along the stone path to the door.

The inside of the house was just as stunning as the exterior: the entire first floor, open and spacious, boasted the same beamed, cathedral ceiling as the guesthouse. As she passed the living room, she noticed a lot of antique firefighting equipment and pictures prominently displayed. "You're an antiques collector?"

"Just firefighting stuff. One of my ancestors started Colter Equipment, a big producer of firefighter equipment and gear, and it's one of the major manufacturers now. I like to collect the old pieces and advertising from the company. It's a hobby. I'm a volunteer firefighter."

Hope smiled as she followed him into the kitchen, not the least bit surprised that Tate was active in helping his community. "The house is gorgeous."

"The kitchen is a waste," Tate grumbled as he brewed her a single cup of coffee, and then started his own. "I don't really use much except the microwave and the coffee maker."

Hope took a seat at the kitchen table as she looked appreciatively around the large, spacious kitchen with every modern convenience and decorated beautifully with granite countertops and cedar cupboards. She took the cup of coffee from him. "Too bad. It's a cook's dream."

Tate dropped some cream and sugar on the table before he grabbed his own coffee. He turned the slatted, wooden chair around and straddled it; his forearms rested on the table. "So are you really okay?"

Hope shrugged. "For the most part…yes. I guess I still have some things that will never go away."

"I don't think you can experience something like that and not have a few hang-ups," Tate observed, his voice low and soothing. "What are you going to do about Jason? You should tell him, Hope. He knows about your career."

Her eyes narrowed. "Thanks to you," she chastised.

"He would have found out anyway. Your portfolio was there. He isn't stupid. He would have figured it out, even if I hadn't helped him. You're married to him, Hope. You need to tell him everything. The guy is crazy about you."

"He's really not," Hope denied. "He wanted to keep me from marrying a man who didn't even exist."

Tate grinned. "The fake boyfriend?"

"How did you know?" Hope added cream and sugar to her coffee and took a long sip, savoring the rich flavor.

"Because I'm not Jason. The guy's not thinking right at the moment. It wasn't hard to figure out, but it took me awhile. I think I finally figured it out when there was no email or information on him in your computer."

"So you didn't think you needed to tell him about that?" She shot him an annoyed look.

"Nah. I figured you'd fess up eventually."

"I told him almost everything. There are just some things I don't want to talk about. I still have a few…issues." Hope sighed. "I can't stay married to him."

"We all have issues," Tate grumbled. "The only way you can resolve this with Jason is to talk to him. Believe me, he wants more than to get into your panties," Tate told her bluntly. "If that's all he wanted, he could have gotten a piece of action with another woman without all that effort."

Hope knew that, and she still didn't completely understand Jason's motivation. She was fairly certain the only reason he stuck to his guns now was to keep her from doing anything dangerous. "Then why didn't he?" she asked desperately. "Why didn't he just find another woman and walk away from me in Vegas?"

Tate crossed his arms over the back of the chair and stared her down. "I think that's something you'll have to figure out for yourself."

Hope let out an exasperated breath. "I know I should tell him. He's confused by some of my fears. He knows everything else. I just have a hard time...reliving it."

"As difficult as I know that will be, I want you to be able to move on completely, which means confronting Jason, letting him know the whole truth," Tate said solemnly, picking up his coffee.

"Me too. I want to move on." She wished she had Tate's confidence so she could be completely whole again. She had thought that she was doing well...until she'd seen Jason. He made her yearn for things she hadn't ever missed before. Last night, and her experience with Jason during the holidays, had been telling. There were still some ghosts she apparently hadn't exorcised.

"How long are you staying?"

"Two weeks. He's blackmailing me," Hope told Tate unhappily.

Tate smirked. "Smart man. He threatened to tell your family if you leave?"

"Yes."

Tate chuckled.

"Tate?" Hope said quietly.

"Yeah?"

"You're kind of a jerk," she told him.

He smirked. "I never claimed to be anything else, darlin'."

Hope rolled her eyes. As much as she owed Tate, he annoyed her with his vagueness. She supposed that came with the territory of being Special Forces. "Are you out of the military?" she asked curiously.

He nodded. "Over a year ago."

Mercifully, Tate dropped the subject of Jason. She and Tate made small talk until they finished their coffee and he walked her back the guesthouse.

She gave Tate a hug on the doorstep as he departed, just as Jason flung open the door.

Chapter 6

"I'll give you two seconds to take your hands off my wife before I kill you," Jason growled angrily.

Hope immediately leapt out of Tate's friendly hug, startled when she saw the murderous expression on Jason's face as he stared at Tate.

"She was out wandering around in the woods. Maybe you should take better care of your wife," Tate answered smugly to deliberately provoke Jason.

"Bastard," Jason grunted as he tried to get around Hope to get to Tate.

"Stop," Hope squeaked loudly. "Jason, I need to talk to you." She stayed between him and Tate and pushed against Jason's chest. "Tate, thank you for walking me home, although I could have found my way back quite easily."

"I think it's becoming a habit to get you back home safely, H.L. Sinclair," Tate answered enigmatically. "I told you he cares about more than just sex," he added quietly before he turned around and walked back toward the path to his house.

"What the fuck did he mean by that?" Jason rumbled. His sapphire eyes shot fire at Tate's back.

"Nothing," she hedged as she tried to push Jason back through the door. She'd made some decisions on her walk back from Tate's house, and she wanted to talk to Jason, needed to try to explain. If she did, maybe he'd agree to help her become whole again. If she didn't try, she'd have to live with the regret of never knowing what would have happened had she asked for Jason's help.

And she'd lived through more than enough things she now regretted.

Turning abruptly, Jason stormed back into the house.

Hope let out a relieved breath, and walked behind him and into the house. She hadn't been quite sure Jason wasn't going to follow Tate. She closed the door behind her and followed Jason into the living room.

"Talk," he demanded. He sunk into a leather recliner, his expression stormy. "Tell me how you end up making out with a guy you just met. Jesus, Hope. What the hell is wrong with you?"

"I wasn't making out with him," Hope answered indignantly. "I was hugging him. And I didn't just meet him today. We've... met before." She dropped her camera and the case carefully on the coffee table and sat on the couch across from him, drawing her legs beneath her.

You can do this. Just tell him. Jason's the only man who can help you right now.

"How in the hell did you meet Colter? He never said he knew you. Were you sleeping with him between boyfriends and breakups?" Jason exploded. His expression grew cold. "I don't get you anymore, Hope. One minute you're freaking out over foreplay, and the next morning I find you wrapped up in another man."

"I know." Hope knew her behavior confused him. Putting herself in his shoes, he probably thought she was psychotic. "I'd like to explain. Please."

"I wish somebody would," Jason grumbled, his expression irascible.

Hope took a deep breath. "I knew Tate by the name of Colt. It's what he used as a code name when he was in Special Forces. I didn't know he was here, or that he was one of the Colorado Colters. He and his Special Forces team saved my life three years ago." She saw Jason open his mouth to ask a question, but she held her hand up, anxious to get her story out before she caved. "Just let me tell you the story first."

Jason nodded, not saying a word as he stared at her darkly.

Hope continued, "I was only a year into my career, and still trying to make a name for myself. I was just starting to get a foothold by taking pictures of extreme weather. I knew there was a cyclone that was going to hit on the coast of India. I got on a plane alone and traveled there, setting myself in a safe place on high ground. The storm was worse than was predicted, and the coastline became a disaster. I was safe, but the damage was enormous, and everything was very chaotic. No one really noticed when I was pushed into the trunk of a car and taken away."

Hope started to breathe heavily, but kept talking to get everything out. "I was terrified and everything was dark for what seemed like days, but it was only a few hours. When the trunk was finally opened, I was far away from the coast and had been taken into a broken-down house outside of a village at gunpoint." Hope shuddered as she remembered the stone cold, emotionless look in the foreign man's eyes, but she shook it off. "There was a...man. I wasn't sure what was happening at first and I begged him to let me go before the authorities found out. He spoke broken English, enough to understand what I was saying. He just laughed, and he kept laughing while he...he..." *Oh, God. Just say it!* "He raped me, Jason. Several times. I fought him, I screamed and tried to get away, but I couldn't. And it hurt. It hurt so badly. After a while, everything got pretty foggy. He beat on me to shut me up, but nobody came to help me."

The tears flowed down her face as she went on. "I think he planned on killing me, but I told him if he contacted the American Embassy he might be able to get some money if he kept me alive. Between—" Hope's voice cracked, but she finished, "Between assaults, he contacted them, and the embassy stalled for time. Tate's unit was there in

India. I found out later they were really close by, actually tracking this particular man because he was a well-known terrorist hiding out in India. I think they knew their best chance was to attempt a rescue because he was going to kill me either way, whether they paid money or not. Tate's team stormed the house and killed the terrorist while I was still alive. They saved my life." Hope sobbed and tried desperately not to remember the pure terror she had felt that day, but failed miserably.

"Tate stayed with me all the way back to the States, talking to me, trying to help me. I never saw him again after that. I never even got a chance to thank him. I was grateful to see him today, happy to get a chance to thank him for what he and his team had done for me." Hope didn't look at Jason. She couldn't. "I went through two years of counseling. The military treated me for my injuries. I had to be tested for HIV at three months and again at six months, and they were negative, thank God. There was never any case to pursue. Tate killed the man who assaulted me, and I thought I was over the incident...until I saw you again. I wanted you, Jason. My body came alive with something I've never experienced before. It isn't that I'm not willing. I'd like to know what it would be like to be with you. I just emotionally...can't." She closed her eyes.

Hope suddenly felt her entire body being lifted up, as Jason sank into the couch and lifted her onto his lap. He ran his hand over her hair and kissed her forehead. His other hand ran up and down her back soothingly. "Christ! I'm sorry, Peaches. I didn't know. I never imagined—" His voice broke, pain and anger both evident in his tone.

Hope buried her face against his shoulder. "I'd never been with a man willingly. I'd never wanted anyone enough."

"You were still a virgin when it happened," Jason stated in an anguished voice. "Fuck. I wish I could dig the bastard up and kill him again." His voice started to vibrate violently, and he buried his face in her hair. "I'm sorry, Hope...so damn sorry. I should have fucking known something was wrong. I was too tied up in my emotions to see you. And I hate myself right now for that," he choked out, his hold on her tighter. "I hate that you went through that all alone. Goddammit! Why wasn't I there? Why wasn't I there for you then?" He rocked her on his lap as his body quaked with emotion.

"It wasn't your fault." She let him comfort her, keep her safe in his arms. She hadn't reconnected with David then, and they hadn't been close. It felt so good to have someone, especially Jason, finally give her solace. Even though she was reliving the horrifying experience, she felt secure in his arms. "Nobody knew. It was a top-secret mission; there were no witnesses and the Indian police never found out. Only the American Embassy and the government were involved. It was an isolated area outside of a village. It was never leaked to the media, and I was grateful for that." It had been horrifying enough without having to deal with a media circus.

"But you needed somebody then, sweetheart. You were all alone, damn it," he rasped as he buried his face in her hair. "I've been a major bastard to you, Hope. I never knew. I never knew." He rocked her harder, his grip on her body clingy and desperate.

The agony in his voice made Hope tremble and feel the volatility of his regret. "You didn't know. And I'm glad you're here now. I was alone, and it was hard. It's easier now."

"I won't make you stay, Hope. And I'll never threaten you again. I'll do anything to make this up to you."

Her heart clenched and she threaded her hands through his hair, giving him back the comfort he gave her so readily. "I want to stay."

"Thank fuck," he growled protectively. "I need to be with you. I want to show you I'm not an asshole all the time."

Hope smiled through her tears. "I know."

"You're not going to be alone. I'll always be there for you from now on. Jesus, you've handled way too much on your own." His body still quaked, and he still rocked her gently. "You need somebody, Hope. Let me be that man. Please."

She didn't just need *somebody*; she needed *him*. Instinctively, she knew that Jason was exactly what she needed. "I'm scared," she admitted hesitantly.

"Christ. I'm sorry. The last thing I want is for you to be afraid of me. I just wanted you to want me," he admitted huskily.

"I do. You're the only man I've ever wanted this way. But hopefully you can understand that my fears took over. It wasn't you I was rejecting. It was the act itself. I get flashbacks when it comes to actually being...penetrated. Or confined." She was blunt. She needed to be for him to understand.

"I won't touch you sexually again. I swear."

It was the opposite of what she actually wanted, and somehow she needed to explain. She opened her mouth to tell him, but closed it when he spoke again.

"You could be dead. Just the fact that you're here is a fucking miracle, that I can hold you like this."

"I lived, Jason. I'm grateful for that."

"You went back into the field again. Why?" He lifted his head to force her gaze to his, his expression still tormented.

Hope stared into his turbulent, troubled eyes. "I had to," she confessed. "I went into a bad depression for a few months, terrified to leave my condo, scared of almost everything and everyone. But I finally decided that I couldn't let him win. He told me he hated Americans; he spit on me. In the end, I needed to spit on those memories, to bury them. He was dead and I was still alive. I needed to really live, not just exist, in order to beat him. It was hard to go back, to travel again. But it got easier. I desperately needed to take my power back again, and I did when it came to doing my job."

Hope took a deep breath, ready to try to explain what she wanted. "It's just that I can't seem to actually have sex. Honestly, I never even tried until you. There wasn't a man who made me want those things. I think it's the thought of being...invaded that freaks me out. All I remember is the pain, and it throws me back there again. Honestly, I haven't wanted to do anything until you. I want you to help me, Jason. Help me get over my fears." If Jason couldn't do it, nobody could. She'd decided to ask him for help on her walk back to the guesthouse. She needed to get past her fear now that she knew that it was there, and the only man she wanted was Jason.

He gaped at her, concern in his eyes. "Hope, I can't force you after—"

"I'm clean and I'm on birth control. After what happened, I take the Pill faithfully because I still travel internationally, and I know what can happen. Maybe that's still a little paranoid. What are the chances that it will happen again? But it makes me feel safer. I was grateful I didn't catch anything and I didn't get pregnant. It isn't that I'm not willing. I want you to understand that, understand why I went a little crazy last night. You know all of my secrets now. I want to stay with you for the next two weeks and try to get over this. When it's over, we can go our separate ways, no matter what happens." She almost choked on her words; it would be difficult to say goodbye, but she understood that she had to try. She might go her whole life without feeling the way she felt about Jason. This could be her only chance.

"You have to trust me, Hope. Really trust me," Jason said huskily. He stroked her cheek, his eyes cryptic. "Now that I know what you went through, I'm scared, too. I don't want to hurt you, and I don't want you to suffer another minute of pain."

"We don't have any secrets anymore. I trust you. Do you still want me even though I've been...used?" She'd gone through years of feeling dirty and undesirable.

He broke eye contact and pulled her head against his chest. "I think I want you even more. You're probably the bravest woman I've ever known. Tate and his men might have rescued you, but you helped save your own life because you're smart. I just wish I would have known about this sooner. I can't believe you went through all of this and never told your brothers."

"I couldn't. I trust you not to tell them. It won't change anything now," she answered nervously. There was no reason for her brothers to ever know, and she didn't want to talk about it again.

"I'll never give away your secrets," Jason replied gutturally.

Jason asked questions, mostly about her feelings during the entire experience and details about how Tate rescued her, and she answered them, feeling much safer talking about it now that her story was out. He was patient, let her answer in her own time, but kept his arms protectively around her, her body cradled in his lap.

By the time she was done telling him every detail he wanted to know, Hope felt nothing but relief, her conscience completely clean. She relaxed in his arms, feeling safe, her body and mind exhausted with relief.

Jason was in Hell, and feeling very much like the Devil himself.

Coward!

His conscience ate at him after what Hope had revealed, hammered at him to tell Hope that he'd cold-bloodedly set up this complete sham to get her married to him. But how could he do that now, when he desperately needed her to trust him?

Christ! He'd lied to her, manipulated her, accused her of some nasty things that she wasn't guilty of at all. She'd been raped. Repeatedly. Beaten. Terrified. All he wanted to do was fix everything, take it all away. But he couldn't, and he hated himself for that.

Bastard!

Asshole!

Selfish prick!

Hope had suffered through horrors that he couldn't even imagine, and yet he'd never stopped to think that maybe something was seriously wrong with her. He'd been too damn worried about himself, how he could fuck her to alleviate his own needs. Did he think about her needs? No...he hadn't, and he should be shot for being such a self-centered son of a bitch.

She'd been brave enough to spill her own life-altering secrets, and they had turned his guts inside out. He couldn't think about her ordeal or how much she'd suffered—how close she'd come to dying—without completely losing his fucking mind. Just thinking about her trapped in the trunk of a car, taken to God knows where in a foreign country, and being violated over and over again made his entire body shudder with fury. His protective instincts were on overdrive, and he never wanted to let her out of his sight again.

Jason was fairly certain if most people had gone through the ordeal that Hope had suffered, they'd never set foot out of the country again. Yet, she'd gone back, determined not to let that experience take over her life. Jesus. That took guts. Maybe Tate had been right when he'd said that Hope had balls.

Obviously, Tate had recognized Hope, but he hadn't let on that he knew her. That pissed Jason off and humbled him at the same time. Colter had kept Hope's secrets, but Jason wished the cocky bastard had said something, given him some warning about all Hope had been through. Jason knew he'd been a complete asshole toward his friend just because of a hug—and toward Hope, with the sham wedding—and he didn't like himself very much at the moment. Colter had saved Hope's life, and for that, Jason wanted to hug the arrogant Tate himself, thank him for protecting Hope when Jason had failed to do so himself.

She's never been with a man except by force.

Christ! He wanted to be the man to teach her that sex wasn't bad. The only man. Just the thought of anyone else touching her made him tighten his arms around her until she squeaked.

"Sorry." He kissed the top of her head. "I'm feeling a little protective."

I'm feeling a little insane! Okay...maybe more than just a little.

"I don't need your protection, Jason. I need you to fuck me and help me like it," she told him teasingly, tremulously.

Jason nearly growled. For him, both of those things were entwined. He wanted to claim her, brand her as his by fucking her senseless, make her his to protect. He didn't want her to remember anything sexually before him. But he was almost terrified of the act himself now. What if he hurt her? Still, if this was what Hope wanted, he would give her any damn thing she desired. "Speaking of protection, you told me you're clean, but you didn't ask if I was," he mentioned gruffly.

"I trust you," she murmured softly. "If you weren't, you would have told me."

Slam!

His conscience bitch-slapped him. Hard!

She trusted him, yet he really wasn't worthy of her trust.

I can't tell her right now. Not yet. She needs to be able to trust me. And from this moment on, I'll never do anything to betray that trust. Someday I'll have to tell her, but I'm going to try to give her what she wants first.

"I'm safe. I've never once had sex without my own protection. I'm not exactly trusting," he admitted honestly.

She wriggled off his lap and sat next to him. Her green-eyed gaze surveyed his face curiously. "How many women have you been with?"

Jason swallowed a lump in his throat and choked out an answer. "Enough."

Hope folded her arms over her chest. "How many?"

Honestly, Jason was ashamed to admit that he couldn't count. "I don't know. I don't remember." He already knew that before Hope, none of them really mattered. They'd been a salve to a wound, a temporary fix, all of them wanting the same thing he did: sex with no strings.

"No girlfriend. Not ever?" she questioned with a small frown.

"Once. When I was in college."

"What happened?"

"She dumped me when she found out I wasn't as rich as she thought I was."

"What?" Hope yelped furiously.

Jason shrugged. "Seriously. She dumped me. I started talking about the problems I was having with my dad's company after we graduated and she left me for a richer man. I guess I was too risky," he told Hope with a rueful grin.

Admittedly, it had hurt at the time, but he'd gotten over it fairly quickly. He'd been too damn busy trying to save the company to worry about the relationship. Maybe it *had* made him cautious and a lot more casual about relationships, but his heart hadn't been broken.

"Nobody would break up with Jason Sutherland." Hope snorted with disbelief. "She must have been insane."

"Am I such a prize, Hope? You're planning on divorcing me." He secretly relished her indignation that some woman had actually dumped him years ago.

"We can annul the marriage. We weren't exactly of sound mind. And this is different. We have an agreement," she answered hesitantly. "She was really your girlfriend. She had no excuse to hurt you."

Jason looked at the ring on her finger possessively.

She's mine. No divorce. No annulment.

Jason's lips twitched as he tried not to smile at her fiery, irritated expression. She was annoyed *for* him, pissed off *for* him. "It was a long time ago." He snagged her around the waist, needing to hold her in his arms again. He settled her back in his lap. "Besides, if she hadn't given me my walking papers, I might not be here right now."

He would be here, and he knew it. Since she was eighteen and he was twenty-three, there had never been anyone else for him except Hope. Maybe he had been biding his time, waiting, but his post-college relationship would have ended anyway. Hope had always been there, in the back of his mind, subconsciously not allowing him to get that serious with anyone else because he could never feel the same way about another woman as he did about Hope. He was exactly where he was supposed to be right now. Finally. He could feel the rightness of it in his gut. The nightmare that Hope had gone through would haunt him forever. His conscience made him wonder whether it might not have happened if he had pursued her before she graduated from college or soon after. No way she would have been running around the world without protection if he had been in her life. And he *should* have been in her life.

"I don't like to think of anyone hurting you," Hope told him softly as she stroked her soft palm over his cheek.

"Now you know how I feel. What happened to you is killing me," he rasped. "I can't take it away, make it go away. I wish I could. But you don't have anything to prove to anyone now. Especially not a dead man."

"I know." She tilted her head and looked at him. "I don't want to be with you for anyone but myself. You're the first man who's ever made me feel alive this way."

Mine.

God help him, but he felt exactly the same way. The problem was, he wasn't certain how to rein things in with Hope. She made him need. Want. Desperately. So primitively and elementally that he wasn't sure he could give her what she needed. "This won't be easy for me," he admitted huskily. "Sometimes I feel like I'm losing control when I'm with you. And I like to have control in the bedroom. With you, I'm almost crazy with the need to hold you down and make you submit to me. I'm obsessed with wanting you."

Hope brushed an errant lock of hair from his forehead. "It's not you. It's me. My body responds to every part of you, especially the alpha, possessive way you take control of my body. It's my mind that's having a problem."

"Then I'm going to need you to stay with me, body and mind, sweetheart. Don't slip away." His eyes roamed over her hungrily. "Respond to me and only to me. See me and only me. Feel me and only me."

Jason saw the look of longing in her liquid emerald eyes and nearly snapped. His dick throbbed to be buried inside her heat.

She nodded and her arms wrapped around his neck. "I need you."

It was the first time in his life he'd heard somebody say those words to him when it wasn't associated with money. Hope wanted *him*, needed *him*.

"You have me." He got to his feet with her in his arms, the most precious thing he'd ever had.

"What are you doing?" she asked curiously.

Jason didn't break his stride as he carried her to the bedroom. "It's time for lesson number one, Peaches, before I go completely insane."

"We have two weeks," she answered, but her voice was low and smoky with desire.

"Not long enough," Jason told her roughly as he lowered her feet to the floor.

Not nearly long enough.

Chapter 7

H ope watched and nearly drooled as Jason stripped the shirt from his body and lifted it over his head. All the muscles in his torso flexed from the action, before he dropped the garment to the floor.

Nimble fingers went to the button fly of his jeans and pulled them loose one by one. His wild, tumultuous eyes never left her face.

Hope gulped as he stripped off his jeans and briefs. They lay on the floor, and he stood before her, beautifully naked. He crawled onto the bed, pushed the sheets and comforter to the bottom. His hands crossed behind his head, and he continued his smoldering look. "You have me. Now what are you going to do with me?"

Oh. My. God.

Sweet baby Jesus, Hope had never seen anything like Jason, all golden skin and crazy *fuck-me* hair lying on the bed as he waited for her.

I've been intimate with him before. I don't need to be nervous.

They had been together, locked lips and other parts of their bodies before, but she still nibbled on her bottom lip nervously. His strong, powerful body and spirit beckoned her, and her core clenched and flooded with liquid heat just from looking at him. His cock was erect, ready, and obviously very anxious. "I was counting on you to tell me how to do it," she admitted.

He shook his head slowly. "You strip. You make your own choices. You're in control, Hope."

It was a challenge, and it was a sacrifice for him. Hope saw his actions for exactly what they were, and it made her eyes moist with unshed tears. Jason was a man of action, a raw, alpha male who gave her control because he wanted her to feel as if she was the aggressor. This was against his very nature, yet he did it for her.

All right, then. I can do this.

She lifted her shirt over her head and dropped it into the growing pile of clothing on the floor. The front clasp on her bra came apart easily, and she let it drop, not even looking to see it land on the ground. She was too busy watching Jason's face.

"Christ. You're beautiful." His voice sounded as if it had been scraped with sandpaper.

As Jason's eyes unabashedly admired her breasts, Hope *felt* beautiful, even though she knew she really wasn't. Her looks were average at best, her curvy figure usually not what men drooled over. Still, her body came alive; her nipples hardened as Jason stared at them as if he wanted to devour them.

"You're all mine for now." She slipped her shorts and panties down her legs, wanting to be with Jason more than she'd ever wanted anything in her entire life.

"Take me then," he replied seductively. "And I've always been yours."

He's the one.

When she'd been in therapy, her counselor had told her that one day she'd find a man who she would trust with her body. Jason was that man, the only male who had ever made her body go up in flames.

"Do with me what you will," Jason agreed, his voice heavy with passion, his hooded eyes moving to her face.

Hope crawled across the bed naked, not feeling as confident as she'd like. Jason was all man, possibly more male than she could handle.

"I don't have much experience with seduction," she admitted as she knelt by his hips.

"Baby, you don't need experience. When it comes to you, I'm a sure thing," he answered. His tone was pained, but his lips twitched with amusement.

Hope smiled weakly back at him, getting lost in his incredible eyes. "I want to touch you."

"Do it," he told her demandingly. "It might kill me, but I'll go out happy."

She straddled him carefully. Her heated core rested at the top of his thighs. With her palms on his shoulders, she stroked her hands all the way down his chest and let herself explore his heated skin. Each defined muscle of his abdomen was traced as she took her time to make her way down to his rock-hard cock. His erection jut up against his stomach. Taking him in hand, she licked her suddenly dry lips as she wrapped her fingers around him and used her index finger to explore the sensitive head. "You're so big," she told him in an awed voice.

Jason let out a strangled groan and gripped the wooden headboard above him with both hands. "You're killing me here, Hope. Kiss me," he insisted in a low, domineering voice.

The demand mingled with a plea in his voice had Hope immediately lowering her upper body over his. She shivered from the feel of his heated flesh meeting hers. Her sensitized nipples abraded against his chest as she thrust her fingers into his hair, every touch heightening her desire.

Their eyes meet and held: fiery blue and emerald green orbs collided, each exuding naked desire. Jason had laid himself bare, left himself raw and open as his hands clutched the headboard harder. His fingers turned white from the effort he made not to take control.

Hope lowered her head and kissed him, poured out her emotions in the embrace. His coarse hair fisted in her hands, the tendrils slid between her fingers; she moaned into his mouth as he took control of the embrace and demanded her surrender, even though she was in the position of dominance at the moment.

Jason's tongue lashed into her mouth, conquered her, consumed her; his hands moved from the wood behind him and wrapped around her. Questing fingers moved up and down her back and down to her ass, touching every available inch of her flesh.

Hope's core clenched hard, as though it begged for his possession. Her hips swiveled against his groin as Jason deepened the kiss, the desperate caress of his lips against hers carnal and needy. Hope felt the same fierce, feral instincts. Her tongue met his with every stroke; the folds of her saturated pussy parted as she ground her hips against him, needing more.

She released a breathy moan as she tore her lips from his. "Please, Jason. I need to feel you. Help me."

His hand slid between them and moved down to the sensitive flesh between her thighs. "Baby, you're so wet," he rasped. He grasped her hair and pulled her head back. "Look at me," he growled. "Don't take your eyes off me. Stay with me."

Hope moved her hands to his chest and used the solid, hard surface for support. "Please," she whimpered. Her need was so sharp as she got lost in his cerulean eyes that she panted.

"Say my name. Say it over and over. Don't you dare close your eyes. Keep looking at me. Know exactly what you're doing, exactly who you're with," Jason insisted. His fingers stroked and circled her clit, the digits saturated with her liquid heat.

"Jason." She moaned, wanted to close her eyes, but kept herself focused on him.

At that moment, there was only the fierce longing for the man beneath her. "Jason."

"That's right, sweetheart. Just me. Only me," he crooned, his expression intense as he placed the head of his cock against her channel.

Hope's fingernails dug into the skin of his chest as he gently grasped her hips.

"It's your choice, Hope. Take me or continue as we are. It's your choice," he rumbled, his hands still on her hips. Waiting.

Take. Take. Take.

She watched as his expression darkened. A muscle in his jaw twitched as he stared at her, ready for her to make that choice.

Wanting nothing more than to give them both what they wanted, she slowly lowered herself onto his cock. The walls of her channel stretched as she accepted him inside her. "Jason." She moaned as she finally sunk down on his shaft.

"Whoa, baby," Jason said huskily and held her hips immobile. "Slowly."

Hope could feel the fullness of him inside her, and she didn't want to go slow. But she also felt a twinge of pain that accepting his large cock caused, and she forced herself to sink down slower. "I just want you so badly."

Inch by inch, her sheath gave way and her muscle relaxed to let him enter. The pain subsided as Jason slowly guided himself inside her, not letting her sink onto him too quickly. His face was contorted, as though he fought for control, but his reassuring eyes never left hers.

Finally, she was completely seated, and his grip on her hips relaxed. As her gaze bore into Jason's, her heart swelled, and her body ignited, the feel of him completely inside her overwhelming and sublime.

"Fuck. You feel so good, baby, so incredibly wet and hot," Jason responded gutturally.

As her body accepted him, Hope let out a sultry mewl of satisfaction. She felt filled, stretched, everything inside her giving way to Jason.

His hands gripped her hips harder. "Fuck me, Hope. I need you."

His plea was her undoing; the agony in his eyes unraveled her. Letting his now gentle grip on her hips guide her, she lifted herself up and sunk back down on him. A throaty groan of satisfaction slipped between her lips and reverberated through the room. Her gaze stayed lock with his, her only need to remove the anguished looked from his eyes, make it turn to one of desire and satiation. Heat coursed through her own body, and she wanted him to give way.

"Are you okay?" he grunted, his voice deep and graveled.

F. A. Scott

"Yes," she hissed. The spiral in her belly unfurled, her body moved with him as his hips rose to meet hers, the slapping of skin against skin hypnotized her. The earthy, elemental joining consumed her, and her eyes fluttered as she rocked against him.

"Keep looking at me. Don't let go. Don't leave me now," Jason growled as he grasped her hair and forced her to keep her eye contact.

"Jason," she murmured with a shaky sigh. As she leaned down to capture his mouth with hers because she couldn't help herself, her tongue thrust into his mouth and mimicked the rhythm of his cock that stroked into her.

He sat up suddenly, never breaking the kiss, one strong hand on her ass as his hips moved up harder, faster, and held her firmly to accept him. Still straddled over his lap, she wrapped her arms around his powerful shoulders, helpless to deny her impending climax. The angle of his thrusts stroked over her clit roughly with every pounding entry; she lost herself to everything except Jason.

Hope tore her mouth from his and tilted her head back as her powerful orgasm ripped through her, unable to do anything except scream his name. "Oh, God. Jason."

"It's me, sweetheart. Only me," he reminded her, his voice harsh and aroused against her ear. Her channel clamped down on his cock, and milked him as he pumped through the spasms with a tormented groan. "Fuck, yeah. Come with me, Hope," he demanded as he grasped her ass with both hands and buried himself to the balls. His own release pulsed as she quivered around him.

Hope's racing heart hammered against his chest as they stayed entwined. Jason's hand stroked up over her back and neck as he held her against him and his chest heaved. "Jesus Christ," he rasped. His body shuddered as he slumped back on the pillow and took her with him.

Stunned, Hope didn't move, didn't speak. She stayed sprawled over his massive, sweat-slicked body, trying to catch her breath.

Finally, Jason rumbled, "Are you okay?"

She was free. Honestly, she felt as if she could fly. "Yes. I'm better than okay," she answered breathlessly. "That was incredible. Is it always like that?" she wondered aloud.

"Never," Jason answered emphatically. "It can be good, but it's never *that* good. We have an incredible chemistry."

Hope smiled against his damp skin. "Thank you."

"For what?" he asked, confused.

"For helping me." Maybe Jason couldn't understand what being able to actually be with a man and finding such ecstasy in an act that previously been abhorrent to her meant. "I finally feel…liberated."

"I'd prefer it if you only explored your sexual independence with me," Jason grumbled.

She laughed delightedly. "Right now, I think you're the only man I *can* explore."

"Feel free to use me for any research you'd like to do," Jason replied hastily. "Please."

Hope finally moved her lethargic body from his and disengaged herself from him to slip next to him with a chuckle. "I'm honored that you'll make yourself available."

He turned his head. His eyes speared her with an anxious look. "Are you really okay?"

Her heart stuttered. The look of concern in his expression touched her. She put a palm to his cheek and stroked his whiskered jaw. "I'm fine. I guess I finally found a man I could trust with my body. I never left you, Jason. Not once. I knew exactly who I was with and who was making my body come apart. I'm not sure I could do this with anyone else but you."

"I don't want you doing it with anyone else but me," he replied roughly, possessively. He wrapped a strong arm around her back as he rolled to his side and brought them face to face.

Their heads both rested on the same pillow and their eyes meshed as they gazed at each other. Hope sighed; her loose hand stroked down his strong shoulder and came to rest lazily on his hip. He might feel that way right now, but he'd get his fill of her eventually, and in return, she'd be finally be free of every ghost of her past. "You'll wear out eventually," she teased.

A low, reverberating sound tore from his throat. "Don't count on it, sweetheart."

The sensual threat and the heated look in his eyes made her heart skitter. Jason's expression was intense, almost feral, as his gaze bored into her. "It might take me a while to get used to it," she agreed. Her body already quickened to have him inside her again. "And I probably have a lot to learn."

"A whole lot," he conceded. "Could take a very long time," he said in a low, *fuck-me-again* voice. A wicked sensual grin formed on his lips.

"We have two weeks," she reminded him.

Jason was silent as his molten gaze swept over her face. "Not long enough."

"That's the deal," she reminded him lightly. Her fingers unconsciously stroked covetously over the hard muscles of his hip and up to his chest.

"Don't push, woman." He slapped her firmly on the ass. "If you do, you won't see the light of day today," he warned her dangerously.

Hope wanted to tell him she wouldn't mind, but he cut off her sinful thoughts.

"You'd be so sore you wouldn't be able to move," he cautioned unhappily.

He was probably right, but Hope didn't want to admit it. "I need to take a shower." She looked back at him after she sat up. "Are you planning on staying in bed all day?"

"Not if you're not here," he answered cantankerously. "It wouldn't be nearly as much fun. I'd rather follow you into the shower."

"I thought you said we had to take this slow," she answered him cheekily as she rose and shot a mischievous look over her shoulder.

"I can still look," Jason answered coarsely. His eyes roamed over her figure with blatant naked desire.

God, he makes me feel like a goddess.

She couldn't ever remember feeling this desirable, and her hips swayed a little bit more as she sashayed into the bathroom.

With a low growl, Jason followed right behind her.

Chapter 8

Hope dug into her purse, ignored the credit card Jason had handed her before she left on her shopping expedition to the town of Rocky Springs, and pulled out her own card instead. She handed it over to the friendly, older man behind the counter, happy she'd found almost everything she wanted, and more.

The sporting goods shop had a wide variety of hiking gear, clothing, and other items that she'd wanted to purchase. Jason had handed her the keys to his rental car hesitantly, as though he thought she was going to run away.

Like I'm really going to leave the man who gives me the most incredible orgasms I've ever experienced.

She wanted more, much more, and she'd shared that little secret with him as she'd snatched the keys, being rewarded with a heart-melting grin and breathtaking kiss before she left the guesthouse.

After she signed for her purchases, she took them to the car, opened the back hatch with a click of a button, and stored them safely in the roomy back of the black SUV. As the door started to close, she smirked as she realized that even though the Escalade was a more expensive vehicle than the one she owned, it was probably the cheapest automobile Jason had ever driven. There was very little need for expensive sports cars in this area, and it was probably the only thing that was available in the small town.

Jason had always liked high-performance vehicles, and one of his hobbies as a teenager had been restoring old classic sports cars. She wondered whether he still did that, or whether he'd dropped the hobby because he could afford any car he wanted already fully restored.

Hope stopped, looked up and down the street, and smirked as she spotted a gourmet chocolate factory. That would have to be her last stop or the chocolate would melt before she got it back to Jason.

Rocky Springs was a lovely mountain town that reminded her of several other quaint, small mountain towns and villages in Colorado. The downtown area, the main street, was a collection of useful and eclectic shops, mostly small businesses and specialty shops.

Not seeing what she wanted, she squinted into the sunlight, trying to see what was across the street.

"You look lost," a friendly female voice said beside her genially.

Hope turned her head to glance at the woman, a beautiful brunette with hair as dark as coal that fell in a long, straight curtain down her shoulders and back. The woman's crimson lips were turned up in a smile, her eyes covered by a pair of black sunglasses that had plenty of rhinestone bling. Whoever she was, she was exotically beautiful, even dressed in a simple red cotton shirt and a pair of jeans, similar to the attire Hope had put on hastily before she left the guesthouse.

Hope smiled back at her. "I'm visiting. I'm staying at the resort, and my—" She hesitated before she continued. "My husband wants to take me out for dinner. I don't have a dress. I was looking for a women's clothing store."

"You're staying with us?" The woman's smile grew wider. "I'm Chloe Colter. I live at the resort." She put her hand out readily.

Hope clasped and shook it. "Hope Sinclair," she answered back automatically. As she withdrew her hand, she surveyed the woman quizzically. "You're Tate's sister." The gorgeous, petite woman looked nothing like Tate Colter.

The woman removed her sunglasses. "The only thing we share is the Colter eyes," Chloe answered with a chuckle as she revealed a pair of the same long-lashed smoky gray eyes as Tate's. "And you're Hope Sutherland now, I understand. Congratulations on your marriage. Tate stopped by yesterday, and he told me and Mom that Jason Sutherland had married and was staying here. We were both dying to meet you."

I actually am Hope Sutherland. At least for a little while. She was still stunned to hear herself called by her married name, and it had never even occurred to her to introduce herself with Jason's surname.

As she recovered from her admission, she realized that looking Chloe in the eyes was like looking into Tate's. "Your eyes *are* exactly the same," Hope replied, surprised.

"All five of us share the same eyes," Chloe replied. "Tate's actually the odd blond sibling, in more ways than one. The rest of my brothers are all dark-haired, like me. He favors my late father. The rest of us all look like Mom." Chloe put her sunglasses back on and pointed across the street. "There's a very nice shop across the street and to the left, a few blocks down. I'll walk with you." As she turned, her head snapped back. "Holy crap! Your ring is stunning."

Hope held up her left hand. "It is," she admitted. "Jason has amazing taste." She squirmed a little as she reminded herself she wouldn't be wearing it for long, but she let Chloe take her hand. The woman turned her hand to different angles to admire the diamond.

Chloe snorted. "Obviously. And we know he has endless funds. But he made a great choice. It's stunning without being gaudy. I'm engaged, so I looked at a lot of rings."

Her eyes automatically glanced at Chloe's left hand. Hope noticed it was bare. "You haven't decided yet?"

Chloe sighed. She dropped Hope's hand and gestured for her to walk with her. "James wants to wait to get a ring."

A startled laugh escaped from Hope's lips. "Your fiancé's name is James?"

"Yes."

"I had a fiancé named James once." Hope couldn't help but laugh as the two women crossed the street. The full force of the Colorado sunshine beamed down on them as they scurried across the street during a break in traffic. She stopped as they arrived under the shade of the awning over the shops on the other side of the road.

"Why are you laughing? You obviously broke up," Chloe asked curiously.

Hope shook her head as they walked sedately down the paved sidewalk. "It's a long story," she told Chloe, her voice laced with humor.

"Tell," Chloe insisted.

As she gazed at the woman next to her, Hope's heart lightened. It felt good to be in the company of another woman who really knew her identity. Other than David, she'd really never had any friends, out of necessity. It was difficult to get close to people when you couldn't really tell them much about your life. She stayed quiet, kept to herself in Aspen. Even her neighbors didn't know who she really was, and it had been a very lonely, very solitary existence.

With a deep breath, she told Chloe the story of her fake fiancé, but only revealed the part about wanting to keep her older brothers from interfering in her life. The other woman stopped occasionally, almost bending over with laughter, and commiserated about being from a wealthy family and having overprotective brothers.

By the time the shopping trip was over, Hope felt as if she'd made a new friend, and it felt incredibly good.

Later that evening, Hope watched Jason from the kitchen—ogling him had rapidly become her favorite activity—as he worked from his laptop on one of the recliners in the living room. He looked deep in thought, his eyes narrowed as he studied what was probably data. She'd cooked dinner and hustled him out of the kitchen to finish whatever he was working on as soon as they'd finished eating. He'd told her he was in the middle of a project, and she'd balked when he'd been ready to go with her shopping earlier in the day. She told him to finish whatever he needed to do while she went to town. He'd given her a look that said he didn't want her to go anywhere without him, and she'd reminded him that it was just a shopping trip. It wasn't as if she was going out to chase a storm. Jason had relented, but he hadn't looked happy about it. In fact, he'd greeted her at the door with a look of relief when she'd returned, and gave her a fiery kiss that had made her body sizzle down to her toes, and every part of her anatomy in between, too.

Hope bit her lip to keep from laughing when Daisy hopped onto the chair and walked over Jason's laptop as though the computer and Jason belonged to her. Her heart skittered as she watched him move Daisy gently, placed the feline next to his thighs, and gave her the attention she obviously wanted by stroking her head and then her silky body repeatedly. Hope grew teary eyed as she noticed Jason murmured to a deaf cat who couldn't hear a word he said. Daisy ate up the attention as though she could hear his comforting words, and bumped him in the belly so he could keep on petting her.

The Jason she adored was back, the caring boy who'd grown into a protective, alpha, kindhearted man. Seeing him, seeing the man he really was, made it even harder to resist him. She hadn't detected any sign of the ruthless bastard who'd tried to blackmail her. Instead, a tear rolled down her cheek as Jason continued to talk to Daisy, moved his laptop and let her cuddle on his lap while he used both hands to stroke her delighted kitty body.

She swiped away the tear, opened the fridge and snatched one of the chocolates she'd stashed away as a surprise.

"I thought most men didn't like cats," she said casually as she sauntered into the living room.

"She seems to like me," Jason said defensively. He continued to pet Daisy as he watched her walk toward him.

She stopped beside the chair. "Open your mouth. I got you something today."

He looked at her cautiously. "If it's a Rocky Mountain oyster, I get to paddle your ass," he warned in a low, ominous voice.

"Hmm...no...it's not. But I almost wish it was now," she pondered aloud before she could censor her words. Something about Jason's preference to be dominating both humbled her and excited her. To let her take the lead had to kill him, yet he did it for her. "Open," she requested sweetly. "Please," she added.

He still gave her a startled but smoldering look from her comment about the spanking. Finally, he closed his eyes and opened his mouth, a gesture of trust that made Hope's heart accelerate. She dropped the milk chocolate pecan turtle into his mouth and watched as he chewed and groaned as the chocolate hit his taste buds. "Good?" She already knew the answer. She had recognized the name of the chocolatier when shopping earlier. It was a small company that had several stores in Colorado, and the chocolates were out of this world.

Jason swallowed, a rapturous look on his face. "Tell me you have more." His voice was both demanding and pleading.

"I have more," she agreed compliantly and smiled. "I know you and chocolate."

"I've had chocolate everywhere in the world, and that's incredible." He lowered Daisy gently to the floor and moved his laptop to the floor beside the recliner.

Hope squealed as Jason wrapped an arm around her waist and pulled her onto his lap. Recovering quickly, she straddled him and let her legs dangle off both sides of the chair. "It's about time I got my turn," she told him with false indignation. "I was getting jealous of my own cat."

He palmed her ass and pulled her closer against him. "I like your cat, baby. But you feel a hell of a lot better." His hand moved up underneath her t-shirt and stroked over the bare skin of her back.

Hope almost purred just like Daisy as Jason's touch shot fire through her blood. She wrapped her arms around his neck. "I can't wait until tomorrow, Jason. I need you." She could feel his hard erection push against the denim of his jeans, and she moved her hips to get her heated, saturated core closer.

I need to be closer. I need him inside me.

"Hope." He sounded tortured as he moved one of his hands behind her head and brought her mouth down on his.

She responded immediately, thrust her hips forward again and tangled her fingers into his disheveled hair to mess it up even more.

Hope surrendered completely and moaned desperately into his mouth as he gripped her ass, trying to mold their bodies together to mimic the actions of their seeking, needy tongues. She actually wanted Jason's dominance, craved having him show her that he wanted her beyond reason. Fear wasn't an issue. Desire reigned supreme, and she was crazed to experience Jason's complete loss of control, to let him show her everything she'd been missing for so long. Hope felt bold and Jason had helped her regain her power. Now, all she wanted was...him.

She pulled away from him, panting. "Fuck me, Jason. I need you."

He let out a strangled groan and stood, her legs still wrapped around his powerful body, his hands still squeezing her ass. "Christ knows I want to, baby. I'm just afraid of doing something wrong. What if it hurts because we're doing it again far too soon?"

Her heart melted as his husky voice, so low and full of passion, also vibrated with concern...for her. "It won't," she assured him. Hope knew in her gut she was right. She knew exactly who she was with, and why she was with him.

"I don't have the control I need with you," Jason protested as he walked them toward the bedroom. "But I'll make you come," he growled. Her feet landed on the floor as he stopped in the bedroom. "Strip," he commanded, his voice harsh with controlled desire.

Hope wasn't having it. She needed Jason inside her. "You do it," she countered and stood back with her hands by her side. "When we made our deal, I told you I'd do anything you wanted. Make me do it," she challenged, without a flinch as she watched his nostrils flare and the muscle in his jaw twitch.

"Why?"

"Because I want you to," she answered in a sultry voice, enthralled as she watched him struggle with himself. They needed to get beyond his fear of hurting her. Her need to feel him raw and untamed pounded at her, her desire to surrender a powerful aphrodisiac. "I know who I'm with. Now do it, Jason," she cajoled, deliberately using his name.

His eyes flared with molten heat, and he raised his hands to the little buttons on the front of her short-sleeved cotton shirt. "Need to touch you, Hope." His fingers fumbled with the first button before he finally gripped both sides of the material and tore it open. Buttons scattered in all directions. Not bothering with the clasp to her bra, he did the same thing to release her breasts as the lacy material gave to his powerful grip.

Hope's pussy flooded with heat as she watched his hungry eyes roam over her exposed breasts. She reached out and clawed at his t-shirt, tried to push it up and off his body. He lifted his arms, let her pull the shirt off and drop it on the floor before he disposed of her bra and tattered shirt as he pulled them down her arms and let them hit the plush carpet soundlessly.

On his knees now, he let his hands roam over her upper body, cup her breasts and tease the sensitive peaks with his thumbs. She braced her hands on his shoulders, closed her eyes and whimpered from the feel of his hot mouth as it left wet kisses on her belly, at the touch of his fingers on her nipples. He sensitized every inch of flesh that he touched, and her body trembled, craving and hungry. "Please," she begged. Every nerve fired with electricity.

Another coil of heat between her thighs built as he pinched her nipples again. He moved his hands down her belly and popped the button of her jeans. The zipper lowered, he grasped the jeans and her panties; his powerful biceps flexed as he yanked them down her thighs.

"Step out of them," Jason ordered gutturally.

Using his shoulders to steady herself, Hope shucked the jeans and panties, and stood before him, completely nude. Her body and mind completely focused on Jason, she wasn't self-conscious. Obviously, he liked her ample hips and ass.

His body lowered more, his butt almost on the carpet. He blew a hot breath over her pussy and made Hope shiver with anticipation.

"Yes," she moaned. "Please." She needed his hot, hungry mouth to devour her.

Running his hands down the outside of her thighs, he brought them back up again on the sensitive flesh on the inside of her legs and brushed against her core. "You're so beautiful," he uttered, mesmerized as he ran his fingers through the cropped hair on her pussy. "This is just as fiery as your hair." His thumb parted her folds and slid through the slick heat to circle her clit.

Hope panted. His hot breath wafted over her core; his teasing finger on her pulsating bundle of nerves was about to make her go up in flames. "Jason," she pleaded.

"That's right, sweetheart. Say my name. Remember who's going to make you come. Hold on to me." He suddenly lifted one of her legs over his shoulder, and then grasped her ass to pull her core against his face and consumed her as though his life depended on her for sustenance.

Sweet baby Jesus! Hope's short fingernails dug into his shoulders as Jason dove into her wet heat and used his entire mouth to ravage her. His tongue laved her flesh, lapped from her channel to her clit over and over, branded her as his own as a strangled cry left her lips, the heat of his mouth on her overwhelming. "Oh, God. Jason. Yes."

Looking down, she felt herself incinerate as she watched his golden head between her thighs, lost in the carnal act of pleasuring her. One hand speared through his beautiful, disheveled hair and she held on, urged him harder, deeper. When his tongue zeroed in on her clit, every flick on the sensitive bud made her body jerk. "Fill me, Jason. Please." She now needed the act he'd performed in the shower that had sent her into a horrifying flashback. There was no doubt she was going to come; her body already pulsated. "Now," she pleaded desperately when she sensed his hesitation. "I need you." She wanted to be completely consumed by him.

He glided two fingers into her, curled them against a g-spot she hadn't even realized she had, and caressed it over and over again.

Hope imploded. Her channel clenched around his fingers as she threw her head back and let her powerful climax take her; her body shuddered as she screamed his name. "Jason!"

He rose and caught her before she could fall. His fingers still gave her every bit of pleasure he could wring out of her. Her head fell forward and landed on his chest. With erratic and heavy breaths, her heart galloped as she held on to Jason for support.

Moving his hand from between her thighs, he wrapped it around her waist, supported her, as his other hand stroked up and down her back. As she regained her equilibrium, he swept her up into his arms and carried her the short distance to the bed to lay her down on top of the silky comforter. She watched as he hastily tore off his jeans and briefs, leaving him in nothing but his golden skin, breathtakingly nude.

Hope's breath hitched as he crawled onto the bed, stalking her. "Once wasn't enough," he told her in a graveled voice. "There's nothing better than hearing you scream my name while I'm making you come."

God, he was magnificent, as feral and wild right now as Hope had wanted him to be. "Then fuck me," she told him in a tremulous voice. She needed all that was Jason, wanted him exactly as he was now.

He moved between her thighs and covered her lower body, his mouth against one of her breasts. "Look up. Remember exactly who you're with right now, baby."

Hope obeyed; her eyes moved from the top of his blond head to look up at the canopy of the bed. She was startled when she saw her own image about to be ravaged by Jason.

Chapter 9

"**O**h my God. What did you do?" Hope was stunned as she stared at the erotic image of herself and Jason naked and entwined on the bed. She knew the mirror hadn't been there before, and it looked suspiciously like the large mirror on the wall in the bathroom.

Lifting his head, he shot her a wicked, wicked grin. "I don't want you to ever forget who you're with again. It seemed like a good way to remember."

"Is that the bathroom mirror? How?" Hope's heart thundered as she looked at Jason's naughty expression. He'd done this for her, and that fact nearly made her come unraveled. All because he didn't want her to have a flashback or remember bad things. Her heart clenched.

"It is the bathroom mirror. And it's very secure. I'm good with tools," he replied with an evil grin. Sobering slightly, he added, "Now all you have to do is keep your eyes open and look up."

Hope tried to swallow a lump in her throat, and she failed miserably. Jason had done this while she was out shopping, neglected whatever work he'd had to do, just for her. His objective was to make her always feel secure, and the fact that he'd gone to that much trouble to help her overcome her own fears overwhelmed her emotionally. "Thank you for doing this for me." Maybe it wasn't necessary, but the act was done out of concern. She wasn't afraid anymore, and she knew she wasn't going to forget who she was with as long as it was Jason.

His clear, blue eyes met hers; green and blue gazes clashed and held for a long, breathless moment as though they were both lost for words until Jason's deep, sincere voice replied, "I'd do anything for you, sweetheart. I can't take away what happened, but I'm sure as hell going to try to erase the memories and replace them with something better."

You already have.

Hope wanted to reply aloud, but all she could do was urge his head to her breast, wanting to sink into him, be surrounded by his essence until she was drowning in him.

She watched as he took one nipple into his mouth and teased it with his tongue, the already hard tips impossibly stiffening even more as every touch of his hot mouth radiated down to her core. He alternated, teased one breast before he moved to the other. Hope fisted her hands in his hair. "Enough," she said breathlessly and urged him onto his back by twisting her body. She couldn't feel, couldn't watch him pleasuring her for another second without having him inside her. "Do you like to watch?" she asked him silkily as she straddled his thighs.

"Watching you do anything has become an obsession for me," Jason grumbled.

Hope stretched her legs out, forced him to open his thighs to let her rest between them. "Then see if you like watching this," she suggested. Her head lowered to leave openmouthed kisses on his chest; she flicked her tongue over his flat nipples as she worked her way down to his sculpted abdomen and traced every muscle with her tongue.

"Fuck," he rasped as she finally grasped his cock and wrapped her fingers around it.

Hope bit back a grin as she flicked her tongue over the tip, tasted the salty moisture coating the head, and circled her tongue along the rim. Jason released a strangled groan; she knelt down, her ass in the air, and lowered her head again to stroke the entire underside of the shaft from root to tip. "How does it look?" she asked, poised to take him into her mouth. Watching him pleasure her had been unbearably erotic, and she wondered whether he felt the same way. More than anything, she wanted to give him the same ecstasy that he'd given her.

"Watching you go down on me is like watching one of my wildest fantasies happen in real life," Jason groaned. "You're killing me."

She wrapped her lips around him and sucked him into her mouth, taking as much of him as she possibly could.

"Holy fuck! Hope." He buried his hands in her hair to guide her head to move on him.

She got drunk on the taste of him, and from the knowledge that with every touch of her mouth on his cock, Jason had the same pleasure she had gotten from him. The realization she could inflame this beautiful man was exhilarating, powerfully intoxicating.

"Need to be inside you now," Jason growled. He lifted her from his body and flipped her onto her back. His chest heaved; his face feral and his eyes wild, Jason pinned her hands to the bed and entwined her fingers with his. "Mine. You're mine. My wife." He turned her left hand so she could see it in the mirror. "No man will ever fucking touch you again without ending up dead," he vowed roughly.

Hope stared up at him, her eyes wide, but not with fear. She felt scorched, his molten skin against hers almost unbearable. "Fuck me, then. Make me yours." She wrapped her legs around him; her heels dug into his ass, urged him to take her. "I need you."

"Are you okay? I'm sorry. I told you I had no fucking control when it comes to you," Jason grunted and moved his weight from her.

"Don't you dare leave me." Hope tightened her legs around him and clenched his fingers that restrained her hands. "You put a ring on my finger. Now make me yours. I don't give a damn how long it lasts. Make it real, Jason. I can see who I'm with. I'm with my husband." Her eyes looked at him pleadingly, wanting him to not feel inhibited by her earlier flashbacks. Jason was possessive of her right now, and it seemed as if prodding that possessive streak was the only way to set him free. "If you don't, maybe I'll eventually meet some man who will."

His expression turned from one of concern and passion to one of almost raw possession. "You. Are. Mine." He turned her left hand until he could see her ring. "Mine. Look up," he demanded, letting go of her right hand to position his cock and sheath himself inside her in one forceful thrust.

Hope moaned as Jason filled her. The walls of her channel stretched to accept him. She did look up, not to remind herself of who she was with, but because watching him take her was the most erotic thing she'd ever seen. Her diamond winked at her, reminded her that for that moment, she *was* his, and she reveled in his possession.

Her nails scored the back of his hands as she gripped them tightly and raised her hips to meet every one of his dominant thrusts. His cock moved smoothly in and out of her saturated core. Fascinated and painfully aroused, she watched them in the mirror, enthralled as Jason pistoned in and out of her, frenzied. His splendid body covered hers covetously, and the muscles in his incredible ass flexed with each powerful, claiming stroke of his cock inside her.

"Jason," she moaned. Her body unraveled. Surrounded by his fierce, fevered essence, their bodies strained together carnally, about to go over the edge together.

"Come for me," he groaned insistently. "Come *with* me."

He lowered his head and kissed her; his mouth devoured hers demandingly. Incessantly. Wildly.

Hope's climax hit her hard and fast, slammed into her body in pulsating waves. Jason tore his mouth from hers and tilted his head back. The muscles in his neck strained as he let out a hoarse groan; her sheath milked him as her uncontrolled contractions clasped and released his cock.

"*Fuck!*" Jason released the curse as he rolled, letting her untangle her legs and rest on top of him. "I lost it. I'm sorry."

"I'm not," she replied breathlessly. "I think you cured me."

He let out a heavy breath of relief. "You drive me completely insane, woman. I can't keep a clear thought in my brain when I'm with you. You're so damn responsive that I lose my head."

Hope smiled against his damp chest. "You're a hard man to resist," she teased.

"I'm your only man," he replied ominously as he swatted her on the ass. "If you even talk about another man again, even a supposed future one, I won't be responsible for my actions. I don't share. Ever."

Hope almost reminded him that they were only a temporary couple, but her heart wouldn't let her say it. Even if she was only his wife temporarily, she wanted to live for today. And *today*, Jason Sutherland belonged to her. She'd worry about the separation when it happened. Just for now, just for once, she wanted to bask in the joy of being with Jason, the only man she'd ever wanted. It was good to feel wanted, and for the first time in her adult life, she didn't feel lonely. Jason filled all the empty spaces in her heart, and even if it was only for a little while, she felt marvelous. "I can't believe you stole the mirror from the bathroom." The thought of Jason disconnecting the large mirror from the wall and attaching it to the bed so she wouldn't be scared was probably the most protective, sweetest thing anyone had ever done for her.

"I didn't steal it. I'll put it back. I told you I'm good with tools, and I found a whole toolbox in the storage closet." His voice was lazy and amused.

"Do you still work on restoring cars?" She wanted to catch up on everything Jason had done in the last eight years.

"When I have the time. I have a shop in New York. I'm working on a sixties Ferrari right now."

Hope could hear the excitement in his voice, and she was glad he hadn't given up something he'd loved. "So you do get out of the city occasionally," she commented jokingly. "Is working on cars your only escape?"

"I get back to Boston as often as possible to see Mom, and I have a boat docked in Boston Harbor. I think my real escape is getting out on the water. It's easy to leave business behind out there."

Hope propped her head up on his chest. "A boat or a yacht?" She doubted that Jason had a regular power boat.

"I guess she's considered a yacht."

"She? What did you name it?"

Jason was silent for a moment. *"Sutherland's Hope."*

She was quiet for a moment, tried to digest the fact that his boat had her name. Obviously it was a coincidence, but it made her breath catch and her heart skitter anyway. "That's a beautiful name," she told him honestly. "What were you hoping for when you named her?"

"Peace of mind." Jason's eyes drilled her with an intense stare.

"And did you find it?"

"Not yet, but if you'd come out on the boat with me, I might," he answered, deadpan.

"I don't have much experience with boats, but I'd love to go." Too bad they wouldn't be together long enough for her to see Jason relaxed and happy.

"You don't need experience. I have a captain and a crew. You just need to make sure you don't fall overboard," he answered gruffly.

"Do you fish?"

"Hell, yeah," Jason answered emphatically with a grin. "What's the point of having a boat that big if I can't fish?"

Hope smiled back at him, enchanted by the thought of Jason actually enjoying something other than business. "How many women have you taken out with you?" Okay…her green-eyed monster had made her speak before she could stifle the revealing words.

"None. Not ever." Jason rolled her over on her back. His body covered hers as he pinned her wrists over her head and looked down at her intensely. "Are you actually jealous?"

She averted her eyes away from his face. "That would be silly, wouldn't it? We're friends. You're trying to help me. We'll only be together for a short time."

"You didn't answer my question, woman." He turned her face back to center. "Tell me," he demanded.

Their eyes met; green clashed with blue, and Hope fell into the fierceness of his stare. "Okay. Yes. A little. Maybe I don't like to share either."

His expression changed. The glimmer in his eyes turned possessive. "Good." He immediately swooped down to kiss her, his embrace full of hungry, delicious need.

Pulling his mouth from hers, he placed tender, openmouthed kisses on her face, her cheeks, down her neck. "You'll never have to share, sweetheart," he comforted, his voice muffled against her neck.

Hope sighed, his words so sweet that she wanted to hold them in her heart forever. But she knew better. Their time was limited, every moment stolen.

"I'll take you out on my boat with me, and we can christen the two cabins. I've never had sex there. She's a complete virgin." He nipped at her neck possessively.

Hope whimpered with desire, her emotions on overload. It felt so good for Jason to talk about a future, but it hurt to know those things would never happen.

But I can be happy for now.

Pushing aside her depressing thoughts, Hope wrapped her legs around Jason and surrendered to his persuasive seduction.

Chapter 10

Two days later, Jason scowled at the shirt on the bed, one that Hope had bought him on her shopping expedition. He loved the hiking boots she'd gotten him, and his woman had been considerate enough to treat them with some water-resistant spray, but he wasn't wearing a damn Broncos t-shirt. He picked up the orange and blue cotton shirt as if it were a poisonous snake. "I'm not wearing this shirt." Hope was in the kitchen, making some breakfast before they went out hiking, and he bellowed loud enough for her to hear him.

She was at the doorway of the bedroom a few seconds later. Jason immediately got as hard as a rock as she looked him up and down. Her eyes lingered on his bare chest. "Hmm…that's too bad. Personally, I don't find anything sexier than a man wearing a Broncos shirt. You'd look very hot. I'm not sure I could keep my hands off you." She sighed, sounded beleaguered, and walked back to the kitchen.

Fuck! He was so going to wear the damn shirt after that comment.

Yanking it over his head, he pulled the stupid thing down to cover the waistband of his jeans. If was going to look hotter to Hope, he'd probably do just about anything. Yeah, he knew she was manipulating him, but he didn't give a shit. Making Hope happy and keeping her turned on had become his primary mission in life.

They'd rarely gotten out of bed in the last few days, and had left the house only once so he could take her out to dinner at the resort. The food had been excellent, but all Jason had been able to think about was the low-cut bodice of her sexy red dress, the amount of exposed skin that he wanted to explore with his hands and mouth. He had even skipped a chocolate dessert when Hope refused anything for her own dessert course, not able to get her back to the house and into bed fast enough for his liking.

He scowled at the credit card Hope had left on the dresser of the bedroom, unused. She'd paid for everything herself on her shopping trip, a fact that both touched him and irritated him at the same time. He wanted to take care of her, give her whatever she wanted. Most women would have taken the card and charged until it was maxed out, which might have taken some time. His limits weren't exactly average. But not Hope. Hell, no! She hadn't used it at all, but left it quietly on the dresser. Sure, she had money, but he had a hell of a lot more, and she wasn't exactly maximizing her income from her inheritance. He jerked his wallet out of the back pocket of his jeans and jammed the card in just a little too hard. Receipts and business cards fluttered to the carpet. Snatching them up, he put them back into his wallet and headed out to the kitchen. His stomach growled as he scented bacon.

Jesus. Hope could cook.

It had to be a skill she'd acquired after she'd left home. She certainly hadn't been taught by her useless mother. Jason's gut ached just from thinking about Hope spending her adolescent years with a mother who didn't want her. Most of her life had to have been lonely, even though she had her brothers.

Just like mine.

He was a stupid bastard, waiting to go after the one woman in his life who he really wanted. And now that he had her, Jason was terrified of losing her again. That couldn't happen, wouldn't happen.

He needed to come clean about his plan to marry her, tell her that he'd lied.

She'll hate me.

After she'd spilled her guts about her past to him, guilt had gnawed at his insides about not telling her the entire truth. The only thing that stopped him was fear, a powerful silencer. If Hope knew, he was afraid he'd never have a chance of keeping her forever, which was exactly what he planned to do. The two-week thing was complete bullshit, and he knew it. He'd waited for Hope for what seemed like forever. He was doing his best to get her addicted to him, to them being together. Christ knew he was a complete and total Hope junkie. He couldn't let her out of his sight for very long without having severe withdrawals.

How am I going to deal with her career?

If he wanted her to give it up, she'd be unhappy if she did. However, he couldn't let her throw herself toward danger either. Maybe they could compromise; he'd go with her wherever she needed to go and make damn certain she was safe.

If she forgives me. If she'll actually stay with me.

By God, she would, even if he had to kidnap her sweet ass again. He wasn't living without her anymore. Her refusal to stay married to him was *not* an acceptable outcome.

Mine. She's Hope Sutherland now, and she belongs to me.

As he entered the kitchen, he saw her bustling around near the stove, and he was as stunned as he always was every time he saw her in the same house as him. Her fiery hair was pulled back into a ponytail, and it swayed as she moved gracefully, efficiently around the room.

Jason was mesmerized by her, fascinated by every move she made. His eyes watched her shapely ass as she bent over to pick something up off the floor.

Oh, hell no. She's never going anywhere. Not without me.

His heart thundered against his chest wall, and his palms got sweaty just from thinking about her leaving him.

Not happening.

"Good morning," Hope said cheerfully as she turned around and spotted him. "You're wearing the shirt. You definitely look like the sexiest man alive," she purred as she sidled up next to him and kissed him tenderly on the lips.

Jason grinned. He couldn't help himself. Hope was managing him, and he was completely on to her machinations. But she was so darn adorable that he wasn't about to call her on it. Nope. He wanted to hear her call him sexy, and he'd do whatever it took for him to hear it. Yep…he was just *that* pathetic when it came to her.

He would have snatched her up if she didn't have a hot pancake turner in her hand. Because she did, he settled for what he could get. "What's for breakfast?" He was getting spoiled, and more than likely, he'd need a very long hike after he ate.

"Bacon, eggs, and double chocolate pancakes with Reese's chocolate syrup." She waved her pancake turner and gestured for him to sit as she loaded a plate for him.

Jason salivated. "They have double chocolate pancakes?" He hoped she wasn't messing with him.

"It's a recipe I got off the Internet. It's decadent, but knowing you and chocolate, I think you'll like it," she teased as she set a plate of bacon and eggs in front of him. "Eat these while I finish up the pancakes."

"You're ruining me," he told her honestly as he dove into his bacon and eggs, famished.

He knew she wasn't joking with him about the pancakes. He could smell the chocolate now.

"It's nice," she replied, her back to him at the stove. "I like to cook, but it's more fun when I have someone to share it with."

Her comment sucker punched him straight in the gut. He couldn't see anything but her backside, but he could hear the vulnerability in her voice. There was no way she wanted him the same way he had to have her, but his heart soared at the thought that she wanted to be with him, liked being with him outside the bedroom. He wanted her to share every space in his life. "Baby, have all the fun you want. I'll be here," he replied roughly as he realized how much he wanted to be everything to her. His life had been just as lonely as hers, maybe more, and only Hope had taken away the restlessness, the emptiness that consumed him sometimes. He needed her more than he needed to take his next breath, and he knew it.

She took his empty plate and slid another one in front of him. His stomach rumbled as he eyed the stack of chocolate pancakes that dripped with chocolate syrup, topped with tiny bites of Reese's on the top. After she set two mugs of coffee on the table, she sat across from him with a much smaller stack for herself.

"Holy Christ. Are these for real?" Jason could smell the tantalizing scent of chocolate and peanut butter, and his mouth watered.

"Let me know if you like them," she said with a knowing smile. "It's the first time I've tried these."

Jason didn't hesitate to pick up a fork and dig into the chocolate fantasy, and groaned as he took his first bite. "Amazing," he said between bites, nearly inhaling the stack of pancakes.

Hope ate hers slowly, appearing to savor each bite. "Mmm...almost better than sex," she purred as she licked her fork.

Jason glared at her. "Sweetheart, these are incredible, but nothing is better than sex with you." Okay, she *had* said "almost" but he still wasn't mollified. He paused, his fork halfway to his mouth, to watch her pink tongue lick the chocolate from the utensil.

Jesus! When did watching her lick chocolate become an erotic experience?

She swiped her tongue over the fork one more time, and closed her eyes, a blissful look on her face. "I'm done," she declared and dropped the fork on her empty plate. "I really like the syrup."

Jason shoved the last bite of pancakes into his mouth as he watched her. Damned if she didn't swipe her index finger across the plate, place it in her mouth, and sucked hungrily at the chocolate-covered digit slowly.

His dick pulsated, strained against the denim that kept it confined. "Sweetheart, if you do that one more time, I'm going to give you something else to put in your mouth covered in chocolate, something a hell of a lot bigger than your finger," he growled. His imagination ran wild.

Her eyes flew open and she gave him an innocent look. "Chocolate-covered Jason?" Her eyes grew sultry and met his with a bold look. "Yummy."

She'd gotten him hot and bothered on purpose, and Jason loved it. The fact that she was becoming a damn seductress, so blatantly sexual with him, made him crazed. She trusted him.

Jason's heart pounded as she rose from her chair; her hips swayed as she moved to the cupboard, lifted a bowl from the countertop and slid it onto the table as she stood right in front of him. "Leftovers," she told him in a low, *I dare you* voice that had Jason on his feet in less than a second.

He yanked at her t-shirt and pulled it over her head. The garment had barely hit the ground before he divested her of the rest of her clothes, frantic to have her naked.

"Jason, I don't think—"

"Don't think," he demanded as he surveyed her standing in front of him, naked. "And don't play with a fire unless you plan on putting out the flames, woman."

"Fine. Get naked." She crossed her arms across her chest. "I was actually planning on using that chocolate syrup on you."

She didn't have to ask him twice. Jason undressed as she stood there and watched him, almost as if she was amazed that he was actually stripping. When he was nude, his cock at full attention and begging for relief, he grinned at her.

Hope might be fearless, but she still looked uncertain due to her inexperience. That made him even hotter. She could tease the hell out of him any time, and he'd show her how to satiate both their needs. He dipped his hand into the bowl and drizzled the warm, liquid chocolate onto her shoulders, smeared some over her neck before he swiped a generous amount over each of her hardened nipples. He let it drop onto her belly and then rubbed it onto her inner thighs and all over her pussy. "Chocolate-covered Hope." He made a low, reverberating sound as he covered her lips with his chocolate saturated fingers. "I think this just became my favorite *fucking* fantasy."

She looked up at him as he smeared chocolate on her lips slowly. Their eyes locked as she opened her mouth and sucked on one of his fingers. Her eyes darkened with desire.

Jason groaned as her tongue swirled over his fingers and licked away the excess chocolate from one finger at a time. She dipped her hand into the bowl and mimicked his actions: swiped chocolate over his lips, down his torso and finally wrapped her chocolate drenched fingers around his cock.

He almost came the moment she wrapped her warm fingers around him. Between watching her suck on his fingers and feeling her warm touch on his cock, he knew he was on the edge. "Hope," he said warningly. He pulled his fingers from the warm haven of her mouth and lowered his head to suck the chocolate from the delicate flesh of her neck. Jason nipped and sucked hard as she moaned and then moved her head to the side to give him better access. He was losing control, and he knew he was definitely going to leave his mark on her, but her breathy pants of pleasure spurred him on. As he moved down her body, he licked chocolate from every inch of her skin and bit gently on each nipple as he laved the chocolate from each breast. The combination of chocolate and Hope made him lose his mind.

Hope reached out and braced her hands on his shoulders as he dropped to his knees and swirled his tongue over her belly. She sunk to her knees with a strangled moan before he could completely finish cleaning the warm skin of her abdomen. Tackling him to the floor, she straddled his legs, her mouth voracious as she lapped at his chest and licked her way down his body.

Jason savored the feel of her lips all over him, closed his eyes and shuddered as her tongue moved over his stomach. If she touched his cock, he was a goner. Sitting up, he lifted her bodily, pulled her to him, covered her mouth with his, and devoured her. His sticky hands released her ponytail and fisted her hair as he branded her as his, losing control as he swept his tongue into her mouth and held her head still to take him. He growled as she speared her hands into his hair, leaned her body into his and surrendered to his brutal possession.

They both came out of the kiss wild-eyed and feral. Erotic need vibrated through the air as he went to his knees, turned her around on his body, and fell back against the tile floor. He pulled her hips toward him until she straddled his face. Her palms came down next to his hips for balance; her mouth hovered over his cock. Jason could hear her whimper as he roughly sucked the chocolate from her inner thighs.

"Oh, God. Jason," she mewled. Her heavy, hot breath wafted over his cock.

He completely lost it as her tongue circled the head, catching on quickly to a position she'd never experienced before.

Fuck!

Knowing he'd come hard and fast, he dove between her thighs and groaned as her liquid heat consumed him. With a tight grasp of her ass, he pulled her down and buried his face in her pussy, lapped at a mixture of the confection he'd smeared on her and her arousal. She was slick, hot, and so damn delicious that he wasn't gentle. His teeth bit gently on her clit; his tongue worked the tiny bundle of nerves like a madman.

He could feel her warm mouth gently suckle his balls, and then, to his surprise, she sunk her teeth into his upper thigh hard enough to leave a mark.

Jesus! She's marking me just like I did to her neck.

The act was so damn carnal and possessive that Jason groaned into her hot flesh. The vibrations dragged a long moan from Hope as she took his cock completely into her mouth, owning it as she moved up and down on the shaft. Her slick hand wrapped around the root of it, unable to take his entire length.

Jason felt Hope's body tremble, and her hips moved. He lifted his hand and slapped her ass hard to make her stop. He needed her pussy in his face, his tongue on her clit. He needed to feel her climax. Now. She moved again and he smacked her ass a second time, feeling the vibrations of her aroused moan around his cock. She knew exactly what he wanted—for her to stay still—and she asked for him to dominate every time she moved. Jason gave her exactly what she wanted, and as he slapped the cheeks of her ass one last time, he felt her body shudder. His tongue speared into her sheath and he could feel her muscles spasm. She moaned desperately around his cock as she climaxed, her strokes against his cock frenzied.

Jason grasped her hips, rubbed his entire face into her shivering folds as he found his own long, hard release and spilled himself into Hope's throat as she continued to consume him.

The two of them lay there on the floor, bodies shivering in completion while they were wrapped together, neither one stopping until they were completely spent.

The kitchen was finally silent except for the sound of their heavy breathing. Hope rolled off his body so he could breathe, and he caught her around the waist to help her crawl up next to him before she collapsed on her belly.

"Best. Breakfast. Ever," Jason said in a husky voice. His chest still rose and fell rapidly.

Hope let out a breathless giggle next to him, and laughed harder as she caught her breath.

The sound of her laughter was infectious, and Jason roared with amusement. He pulled her sticky body on top of his.

"We're a mess," she snorted gleefully.

The kitchen floor was smeared with chocolate everywhere, and Hope's hair and face still had remnants of the sticky sweet dotting her creamy skin. She still chortled with delight as their eyes met, hers filled with joy.

To Jason, she'd never looked more beautiful. He got to his feet and pulled her up beside him, wrapped his arms around her waist and bent down to rub his nose against hers affectionately. He kissed her tenderly, savoring the feel of her in his arms.

As he pulled back, he could see a small red mark on her neck. "Did I hurt you?" he asked, remorseful as he traced a finger lightly over the spot.

"No," she answered with a sated sigh. "I love it when you lose control." She wrapped her arms around his neck. "This morning was so…" She stopped, seemingly unable to find the right words.

"Kinky," Jason finished with a wicked grin.

She nodded and smiled back at him.

"Sweetheart, you haven't seen kinky yet," he told her huskily.

Her eyes lit up. "There's more?"

Jason laughed. Her enthusiastic look amused him. "A whole lot more."

"You'll teach me everything before you go?" she asked tentatively.

"Count on it," he vowed forcefully. He wasn't going anywhere, and neither was she. She was stuck with him, asshole or not, and he hated it whenever she mentioned separating. If he got his way, and he was determined he would, they'd have forever. "And I'm not going anywhere." He tightened his arms around her convulsively.

Happy to finally have Hope in his arms, Jason was still full of regret and remorse. He was a fool not to have recognized how he felt about Hope years earlier, and he might have saved her from the horrifying trauma she'd gone through had he been honest with himself and with her. Fucking her wasn't going to rid him of his restlessness or his loneliness. He needed her, but he had to have her in his life forever. He should never have lied to her, plotted for his own selfish reasons. All he could do was hope she'd forgive him, or she might as well rip his heart out and stomp it into the ground.

Truth was, Hope had him wrapped around her little finger, and Jason wasn't even struggling to get free. If he hadn't been such an asshole, he would have realized that he was completely, totally, and irrevocably in love with Hope, and probably had been since the day he'd seen her at her high school graduation, at the age of eighteen.

In their current situation, his epiphany left him completely, totally—but hopefully *not* irrevocably—screwed.

Tell her the damn truth.

Jason vowed he would. Soon. Very soon.

Chapter 11

J ason and Hope didn't emerge for their hike until three mornings later, when they finally untangled themselves from each other long enough to get out into the early morning sunrise.

Hope took a breath of the crisp, mountain air. Her heart flip-flopped as she centered Jason in the lens of her camera and captured his image with the waterfall as a background. She'd started to photograph him a lot in the last few days, wanting to make sure she would remember this surreal period in her life where she felt wanted, needed, cared for by Jason. Her camera adored him, and every photo she'd taken of him took her breath away. "Thanks," she told him, and lowered her camera. She'd already photographed the falls, and she'd got some incredible wildlife and landscapes as they made the long hike to the place Tate had recommended. He'd sent Jason a trail map, telling him the waterfall was worth seeing, and it was. It was a spectacular sight, the water falling in several different streams from the rocky cliff above. "You're incredibly photogenic," she told him teasingly as she moved up to the edge of the viewing cliff to stand beside him.

He wrapped his arms around her waist and pressed his forehead against hers. "You just want blackmail pictures of me in this Broncos shirt," he accused jokingly in a low rumble.

Hope's heart melted like it always did when Jason was playfully affectionate, which was almost all the time for the last few days. He had to be touching her in some way constantly, and it wasn't strictly sexual. "Maybe I do," she answered mischievously, not wanting to tell Jason the real reason she wanted the photos: so she could look at them when he was no longer a part of her life.

Jason clasped her hand and entwined his fingers with hers. "Ready?"

She nodded. They had a long hike back, and she'd gotten all the photos she needed. "Yes."

Keeping her hand in his, he walked in front of her, down the steep incline, his footing secure as he traveled over the rocky surface.

"You don't look like a novice hiker," Hope mused aloud.

"I'm not, actually," Jason responded. "I started doing some climbing when I was in college. I still go on different climbs with a few of my college buddies."

"You're a climber?" Hope watched her footing as she followed closely behind him. "What sites have you done?"

Jason rattled off several places, some of them pretty advanced courses.

"And you called me crazy for chasing storms?" she chastised. The visions of Jason hanging from a cliff gave her palpitations.

Finally at the bottom of the steep, rocky incline, he reached out and grasped her by the waist and swung her to the grass beside him. "It's fairly safe," he protested. "I take safety precautions."

Hope propped her hand on her hip. "I told you the same thing about chasing extreme weather."

"That's different," he replied, his tone irritated.

"Why?"

"Because it's you taking those risks. Anything could happen to you."

"But it's okay for you to have a dangerous hobby? Taking extreme weather photos is my job."

"It's your choice," Jason answered gruffly. "It's not like you need the money."

"Maybe not. But I'm not incredibly wealthy anymore. I gave most of my money away," she shot back at him. He'd be annoyed, but she didn't care what he thought right at the moment.

His eyes registered his astonishment, and then narrowed as he stared at her incredulously. "Why? You told me you had it in money markets."

She hadn't meant to tell him about the money. Her decision had been personal, and was really none of his business. But they'd grown so close since they'd been here, and she wasn't angry with him anymore. In fact, she knew she was in love with him, and it made her want to share everything with him.

I love him. I love him so much it hurts.

"What I told you is true. I have enough money to keep me comfortable for the rest of my life, even if I can't work. But I've given away the majority of my inheritance to the victims of the natural disasters I've witnessed. It did the victims far more good than it was doing me by sitting around in a bank account." Knowing how financially brilliant Jason was, she knew he'd be disappointed in her lack of ambition to make more money. She pulled her eyes away from his face, and headed down the trail, not wanting to see his reaction.

"Hope." Jason caught up with her, grasped her by her upper arms, and swung her around to face him. "You're the most incredible, sweet, generous woman I've ever known," he admitted in a hoarse voice full of emotion.

She looked at him quizzically, squinting up at him against the sun. "I don't have the same ambitions as you do. I don't care about the money. I'm not stupid, and I've kept plenty to keep me safe. But money doesn't make me happy."

"Then give it all away. It doesn't matter. I'll always keep you safe," he answered urgently. "I have more money than either of us can ever spend. Hell, we couldn't make a dent in our net worth if we tried."

She gaped at him, his expression earnest and sincere. "We aren't staying married, Jason," she reminded him. Her heart pounded so hard she could hear it thunder in her ears.

"I want to. I want us to stay married forever, Hope. I want you with me wherever I go, and I want to be with you wherever you need to travel. I don't want to separate—not in a week, not in this lifetime." He looked at her covetously, pensively.

"You can't be serious?" She wanted Jason more than she wanted anything in the world, but he couldn't really want to stay with her forever.

"I've never been more serious. I don't want anyone else, Peaches. Just you. Somehow, I'll deal with your job. I'll go with you so that I can keep you safe. You can give away my money once yours is all donated if it makes you happy." His low voice vibrated with intensity.

He's serious. He really wants me if he's willing to let me give his money away.

Jason didn't joke about money. Investments and finance were his life. "Really?" she answered tremulously. Her eyes started to tear. "You want to stay married?"

Oh God, please don't let him be teasing me about this.

She knew her heart would shatter into a million tiny little pieces if he wasn't sincere.

He pulled her into his arms, wrapped them around her securely. "I need you, Hope. Please stay with me. I need your sweetness to balance out the asshole in me. I need your huge, generous heart to remind me that not everyone cares about money. I need to be wanted for something other than my bank account. I need you to fight with me when I'm giving you too much shit. And I won't complain about your career." He hesitated before he added, "Well, I'll try not to complain about it too much."

Hope's heart swelled with every word he uttered. She threw her arms around his neck and pressed her face into his shoulder. Her tears fell steadily. "I won't donate your money. I promise." She sobbed; relief coursed through her trembling body. "I think you already donate plenty."

"What's the matter, baby?" He stroked his hand over her hair, his voice confused and concerned.

Pulling back, she looked into his glorious blue eyes and saw…him. Jason left himself wide open and vulnerable, with no attempt to hide his fear. He wanted her that much. "I was so afraid. I didn't know how I was going to live through saying goodbye," she told him bluntly.

"You'll stay with me?" he asked, his voice cautious.

"Yes, you crazy, beautiful man. I want to be with you more than I want anything or anyone," Hope replied breathlessly. "I'm addicted to you."

Jason grinned. "It worked. I got you hooked on sex."

"I'm not addicted to sex," she protested. "I'm addicted to you."

Leaving a firm arm around her waist, Jason grasped her left hand and brought it to his mouth to kiss the ring on her finger. "Then marry me, Hope. For real."

A startled laugh escaped her. "Correct me if I'm wrong, but I think we're already married."

"But you never had a choice. Choose me," he demanded roughly, his liquid blue eyes molten with emotion.

"I wouldn't choose anyone else," she told him gently as she lifted her hand to stroke his whiskered jaw.

"Thank fuck!" He picked her up by the waist and spun her around. "No more talk of leaving me. Ever," he insisted bossily.

"Never," she replied with a happy laugh as she found her footing on the ground again, happy that he had his dominance back again. She had hated seeing Jason vulnerable. If she had her choice, she'd let him try to boss her around for a lifetime. Not that she'd let him, of course. But she preferred to see Jason bold compared to the naked fear she'd seen in his eyes a few moments ago. But God, how that openness had touched her soul. Jason Sutherland wasn't the kind of man who let anybody see his weaknesses. However, he cared enough to show them to her.

"Come with me." He clasped her hand in his and pulled her along behind him. They plowed through the pines until he finally stopped and turned to her. "I need to be inside you, Hope."

She wanted him, too, and she understood what he was feeling. Her core clenched with the need to have him move inside her, giving her assurance that they weren't parting. It was a need that went deeper than physical pleasure, a validation of their agreement to stay together. "Yes." Her body craved to be joined to his.

"You're mine now," Jason said covetously and backed her up against the large trunk of a tall pine. He joined their hands, twined their fingers together and pinned them over her head as he took her mouth with breathtaking swiftness.

Hope gave way to him immediately, opened her mouth to let him plunder, and moaned against his kiss. Her body fired red-hot as she melted into his hard, muscular form, just as needy as him to feel them joined. She met his tongue, tangled it with hers, and let him claim her just as surely as she claimed him.

She came away from the embrace panting. "Now, Jason. I can't wait this time." He didn't need to tease her body. Her core was already saturated, hungry and needy to be filled. "Please."

Jason made short work of her jeans, lowering them to her knees while he opened the front of his own denims. "We don't have the mirror, Hope. I—"

"Oh, Jason." Her heart clenched as she saw the hesitant look on his face. "I haven't needed that mirror since the beginning, although it was pretty hot. I know the feel of you, your scent, and your touch. I'm never going to freak out on you again."

Whirling around, she braced her hands on the trunk of the tree. "Fuck me, Jason. Take me before I die of frustration," she begged, completely unfamiliar with this position, but so desperate for him she didn't care how he took her, as long as he did.

His hands palmed the cheeks of her ass and stroked over them with reverence. "Jesus, Hope. You're so damn beautiful." One hand moved between her thighs, and he let out a low hiss as he was greeted by nothing except wet heat. "You're so hot, sweetheart. I can't wait either."

Hope dropped her head in relief as Jason impaled her, sunk so deep inside her sheath that she cried out his name. "Jason."

"It's me, sweetheart. It will always be me," he reassured her possessively.

Pulling himself almost completely out of her channel, he thrust back in and grasped her hips to keep her steady. Hope squirmed, pushed back against him; she needed more. "Please, Jason. Don't make me wait."

Her pleading tone inflamed him. He started to move; his cock stroked in and out of her saturated pussy powerfully, forcefully. Hope met his every thrust, moved back against him and their skin audibly slapped together from the strength of his movements. "Yes. Harder," she pleaded, needing Jason to give her everything he had.

Moving one hand from her hips, he slid it down her belly and between her thighs, opened her folds until he found her clit. "Come for me, baby. I'm not going to last long," he grunted. His finger stroked blissfully hard over the pulsating bud.

Hope trembled, the feel of him filling her over and over again and the rough stimulation to her clit making her come undone. She splintered, fell apart as her powerful climax took control of her body, crashed over her in waves, and continued on as Jason pummeled into her and found his own release with a strangled groan. "Hope." Her name tore from his lips and he entered her one more time, going as deeply as possible as he spilled himself into her womb. Still inside her as they shuddered against each other, he wrapped his arms around her waist and buried his face in her neck. "My sweet Hope," he said, claiming her aloud.

Hope wasn't sure how long they stayed that way, joined together, basking in the bliss they'd just shared and the intimacy of their positions. Jason finally moved, pulled her up and covered her again, and fastened her jeans before he did up his own. As he pulled her against him, he buried his face in her hair and held her so tightly she could barely breathe, but Hope wasn't about to complain. He felt way too good, and she wrapped her arms tightly around his neck and stroked his upper back in soothing motions, the two of them completely lost in each other.

Chapter 12

J ason was out of time.

He gripped the steering wheel of the SUV a little tighter, his whole body tense. After their agreement to stay together yesterday, regret had churned in his gut, guilt almost eating him alive.

I have to tell her.

He'd never once thought about trying to get away with not telling her he'd set up this whole sham of a marriage. After he started everything out wrong, he wanted to make the situation right. Problem was, he wasn't quite sure how to do it, and he couldn't bear the thought of Hope leaving him.

She deserves the truth.

Hope had lied, but it was nothing that personally impacted his life, or so *she* thought. Plus, she had come clean about everything to him. The secret he kept was personal, and she could very well end up hating his guts for doing it. Hell, *he* hated himself for it.

She's staying with me. I have exactly what I want.

But really, he didn't. *Fuck!* He'd spent most of his life without a single damn insecurity. Even when he'd taken over his father's company and discovered it was nearly broke, he'd believed that he could fix the problem. Now, he couldn't go two seconds without thinking about Hope: how she'd react to learning that he'd actually orchestrated their marriage, whether she was happy, whether she'd get hurt or if she was sad.

Love is Hell.

Jason knew he loved Hope. He'd gotten just as crazy as Grady, and God knew that his friend had practically gone insane over his wife, Emily.

Tell her now; tell her later. Both ways, he was screwed, and he did need to tell her. They weren't going to be happy until he did.

Selfish bastard.

He didn't want to hurt her, not after all she'd been through and how far she'd come toward trusting him. However, some of his hesitance was selfish, his personal desire to not see the hurt look on her face when she found out what he'd done. His own heart would be broken because he'd wounded her—again.

"I'll never lie to her again," he muttered angrily as he pulled into the private drive of the guesthouse.

He'd gone into town to pick up a few things they needed for dinner and left Hope at home because she wanted to preview and organize some of the photos she'd taken the day before. Jason had been gone longer than he'd meant to be: he stopped at the flower shop to buy Hope some flowers, and the jewelry store, the same store where he'd bought their wedding rings before he'd flown to Vegas. He ended up buying a diamond heart necklace, surrounded in diamonds with an emerald heart in the center that matched her eyes. It was the best way to express how much he loved her, and she could wear it all the time. Still not satisfied, he'd ducked into a specialty shop and got her a waterproof camera, hoping to hell she'd be using it for trips out on the boat.

Jason exited the SUV, gathered up everything, and walked the short distance to the house with his heart hammering and his nerves about shot. He'd tell her now, before another minute passed. It wasn't in his nature to put off something unpleasant, something he had to do, which was why his remorse gnawed at his insides. For both their sakes, he needed to get this task over with and rely on Hope's generous heart, her capacity to forgive.

Maybe if she understands that I love her, that I was temporarily insane...

Jason put his key in the door, having locked it before he left. Surprisingly, he found the door unlocked.

I know I locked it.

It had been a priority, and he remembered doing it, not willing to leave Hope vulnerable, even if they were in a small town.

"Hope," he bellowed as he walked in the door. She wasn't in the living room where she had been when he left.

Jason plopped the load he carried down on the kitchen counter, and moved quickly to find her. Finally, he returned to the kitchen. The house was empty.

Where the hell did she go?

As he looked around the kitchen, hoping to find a note, he found something else that made him freeze for a moment as he stared at it. It was the receipt for their rings, a very similar piece of paper to what he'd gotten today when he made another purchase at the same store. How had it ended up here?

It hadn't been there when he left. Jason's heart sank to his feet. The receipt was dated, proof that he'd purchased the rings before he'd left for Vegas. It had to have dropped out of his wallet, probably when he'd put his credit card away.

Hope had obviously found it.

"Shit!"

Running outside, Jason checked around the house. His fear overtook his brain. "Hope," he hollered futilely. There was no sign of her.

She's gone. She left. Dumb bastard. I should have told her.

Not stopping to think, he yanked his cell phone out of his pocket and punched in Grady's phone number.

"Have you heard from Hope?" Jason asked immediately, urgently, when Grady answered.

"No. Not for a while. Why?" Grady asked cautiously.

"We were together and she disappeared. I was hoping she'd call you," Jason admitted. His mind raced frantically to try to figure out where she'd gone.

"You were together? Why?"

Jason took a deep breath and quickly explained what he'd done, and what had happened, not leaving out any of his own less-than-stellar actions. He didn't tell Grady any of Hope's secrets. Those were her secrets to keep...or not.

"You bastard," Grady rasped. "You got my sister drunk in a strange town and forced her to marry you?"

Jason wasn't even going to argue that Hope wasn't forced. She was incapacitated, and he was a dick. "I love her, Grady. I didn't want her to marry another man. Hope is my entire world now, my wife. I need to find her. Kill me later, but help me right now. Please."

"She wouldn't be missing if you hadn't betrayed her," Grady grumbled angrily. He was silent for a moment. "I'll check with my brothers, but they're going to want to castrate you, too."

"Fine." Jason didn't care what anybody did to him as long as he could find Hope. "I'm going to search the trails. She didn't have a car. She couldn't have gone far."

Jason's heart sank as he saw the camera case next to the recliner. She must have been upset. Hope never left the house without her camera.

"You better find her, and you better be ready to grovel."

Jason had never groveled before, but he was willing to do it now. "I'm ready. Call me and let me know what you find out from your brothers." He disconnected his cell and jammed it back into the pocket of his jeans.

A plaintive animal cry came from the door, and Jason looked down to see Daisy twined around his ankles. He picked her up, but the feline still continued to mewl pitifully.

"You're worried too, aren't you?" he asked Daisy, trying to calm the cat by stroking her head, to no avail. "I know exactly how you feel, girl, and I'll find her."

With Daisy back on the floor, Jason tore through the door determinedly, not bothering to lock it behind him.

"Did you know?" Hope asked Tate, furious. She'd been flying high about she and Jason staying together one moment, and the next she'd been devastated. After she'd found the receipt on the bedroom floor for their rings, she was positive that Jason had come to Vegas intentionally to seek her out and marry her.

She'd hiked to Tate's so-called cabin and confronted him; he'd said that he'd flown her and Jason back home. At the time, she'd thought nothing of it because it was perfectly reasonable that Tate had business there, too. Now, she had little doubt that Tate had been there only because Jason needed his help.

Tate frowned. "He didn't tell you. I thought he came clean with everything."

"Why don't you tell me? Obviously Jason isn't talking," she snapped back at him as she seated herself in one of the chairs at Tate's kitchen table.

As usual, Tate flipped his chair backwards and sat across from her. "What do you know?" He looked irritated but resigned.

"I thought he married me when he was drunk. I thought he was there on business and we met completely by accident. I found the receipt for the rings, and it was dated the day before he came to Vegas, and it was from a jewelry store here in Rocky Springs. Why?" She crossed her arms and glared at him.

"We planned everything here," Tate admitted. "Jason was here for the charity ball, and he found out you were getting married. He was desperate to separate you from the guy you were marrying. We made a plan and executed it the next day."

Hope gritted her teeth, hating the cold way Tate had of explaining what they'd done. "So you just didn't fly us back? You were there at the wedding, weren't you?" She was sure of it.

"I was one of the witnesses," Tate replied flatly. "You would have found out eventually because I signed the certificate that went to the courthouse."

Tears sprung into Hope's eyes as she looked across the table at the man who had always been a hero to her. Not only had Jason betrayed her, but so had Tate. "So his plan was to get me married, screw up my engagement and then screw *me* out of his system." She swiped a tear from her cheek angrily. "Why, Tate? Why would you do that when you knew he was just going to dump me later?"

"First of all, I didn't know it was you until we met up for the wedding. Second, Sutherland had no plans of dumping you. The guy was sickeningly crazy about you, always has been. And you were crazy about him, too. Maybe you were drunk, but you weren't unwilling. You looked...happy. I hadn't quite worked out the fake fiancé thing yet, and I didn't want you marrying somebody who would make you miserable either. You deserve to be happy."

"You really thought I'd be happy in a wedding-by-mistake with a man who didn't love me?" she asked him tearfully.

"Oh, he loves you. And you love him, too. Think, Hope. Maybe he's afraid to tell you, but was everything that's happened between you a deception? I don't know Sutherland that well, but I know he spends a hell of a lot of time trying to manage funds for a very large, joint charity for abused women. He was here for a charity ball to help raise money for that organization, willing to make a fool of himself by being auctioned off and be the date of any female who had deep pockets. Maybe he has fucked up with you. But I'm pretty certain he would have told you everything. I think he was afraid of losing you."

"He's never told me he loves me," Hope said forlornly. "He just said he wanted to stay together, make our marriage real."

"Did you tell him?" Tate volleyed back at her. "Everything he's done is because the poor guy was desperate. Do you really think he'd do what he did for any other reason? It's not like he needs to get a woman drunk to have her. But he wanted you, and he wanted you to be his wife."

Hope's heart lifted for a moment, wondering whether what Tate said was true. But she had a hard time accepting that Jason hadn't told her the truth. He'd cold-bloodedly forced her to do what he wanted. "I want to go home." She was still pissed at Tate, but mostly she needed time to think about what had happened with Jason.

"Why? So you can keep running away?" Tate asked furiously.

"I'm not running—"

"Bullshit," Tate said forcefully. "I get that you were looking for freedom and maybe an adrenaline rush when you first started in photography, that you wanted to make a name for yourself by chasing storms. I also understand why you wanted to go back to doing it so the bastard who kidnapped and assaulted you didn't win. But I don't think you're happy doing that anymore. It's your way of staying disconnected. I saw you taking those wildlife pictures, Hope. You were in your element. I have a hard time believing that storm chasing isn't getting a little old, but that you don't know how to do anything else to numb yourself but running around the world, chasing storms. You've disconnected yourself by lying to your brothers, so you can't talk to them. And you're going to run away from a guy who clearly loves you, even though he isn't fucking perfect."

"What makes you the relationship expert?" Hope asked defensively, but she started to think about her days here with Jason. Everything *hadn't* been a lie: the gentleness he showed her, his willingness to help her get over her fears, his comfort when she needed him, even the way he treated her darn cat. He'd lied, but so had she.

"I'm an expert because I'm just an observer. I can see exactly what's going on. Maybe I've never felt that way about a woman, but I can clearly see how both of you feel. Hate me if you want to, Hope, but I thought I was helping you. I'm still trying to help, dammit," he informed her heatedly, running a hand through his short hair in frustration.

"I don't hate you," Hope whispered huskily. "I can be upset with you, and I can be pissed, but I could never hate you. You saved my life."

"That was my job. This is personal," Tate said morosely.

Hope knew Tate was wrong. He'd taken his job very personally. They were one and the same. "I don't hate you," she repeated.

"Good. Because I've always kind of liked you," Tate told her with a grin. "You have balls. Now use them and talk to Jason." He hesitated a moment before he said evilly, "But make him grovel before you forgive him. He should have told you the truth by now. You're married to him."

"Tate?"

"Yeah?"

"You really are a jerk sometimes," Hope told him, deadpan.

"Does that mean you haven't forgiven me?" He flashed persuasive gray eyes at her and his dimple dented his cheek.

"I'll think about it." Hope stood and made her way to the door, knowing she'd already forgiven him. She had no doubt he was being a know-it-all, thinking he had the answers to all of her problems. And maybe he actually did. But she wasn't telling him that. He had a fat enough head already.

Following behind her, Tate mentioned arrogantly, "No woman can stay mad at me. Not even my mother or my sister, Chloe. One minute Chloe's pissed, and the next she's hugging me until I can't breathe."

Hope could believe that. Tate Colter was a real charmer when he wanted to be. As she opened the front door, she turned back to him. "I'm not going to hug you," she warned him.

"You will eventually," Tate said with a shrug. "I'll walk you back."

"No. I'm good." Hope really needed some time alone to get her thoughts together. If she was going to confront Jason, she needed time to think.

"You sure?" Tate asked dubiously.

"I know my way back, and I'm not exactly a stranger to a hike in the Colorado wilderness." She rolled her eyes.

"You want to hug me," Tate told her mischievously.

Narrowing her eyes at him, she shot back, "No, I really don't." Hope closed the door in his face with a small smile.

Tate Colter could charm any woman out of her panties—every woman except her. She was so on to him now. Still, he'd be a hard man to resist for any woman not already in love with another man.

Hope found the trail back to the guesthouse and followed it. Her mind wandered off to Jason, another man who was almost impossible to ignore.

A man I don't want to ignore.

She was hurt, but maybe Tate was right about a few things. She really *didn't* want to go back to chasing storms all the time anymore. She loved doing wildlife photos, and she was ready for another challenge. Years of watching the devastation those forces of nature brought to people's lives had taken its toll on her. Burnout had hit her after a short time back in the field after her kidnapping, and she could have quit then. She'd proved that she could do it. But there had been really nothing and nobody else in her life, and she'd kept doing what she knew. Maybe she had been running away, disconnecting herself.

When she got about halfway home, she veered off on another trail, one she hadn't taken before.

I'm not ready to face Jason yet.

The path was more challenging, the steep, rocky inclines making her pick her way carefully downward.

Lost in her own thoughts, she just kept moving on until the path wove her through some rock formations, and she ended up in a canyon, an area with no other way out.

Her eyes searched for another opening in the vertical rock faces as she walked around the large canyon, but she saw none. She was going to be forced to go back the way she had come in.

"Damn," she whispered, angry with herself for letting her wayward thoughts distract her, make her walk off the beaten paths.

Heading back to the other side of the canyon after finding no escape, her foot slipped on a sloped rock incline, and she went down instantly with a cry of pain.

Sitting up, she stretched out the ankle she had turned going down, the pain almost unbearable. She scrambled to her feet, but she went down again, unable to bear any weight on her injured leg.

She'd left without a cell phone—not that she'd get any reception at the bottom of a canyon anyway. As she crawled to an area without the painful rocks underneath her, she bit her lip to keep from crying out in pain. Planting her ass on a grassy area, she panted and wondered what the hell she was going to do. She wasn't that far from the guesthouse. She'd vaguely been paying attention to the direction she headed as her mind had wandered.

"It's getting there that's going to be the problem," she mumbled to herself.

Trying to rise once more, she failed when she tried to walk, and she had to take off her hiking boot due to the swelling of her injured ankle.

As she saw the size of her ankle, she knew the injury wasn't going to allow her to walk anytime soon. Her options limited, Hope decided she'd rest a few minutes and attempt to crawl back as close as she could to the main trail. She'd have more chance of being found.

Please care enough to be looking for me, Jason.

It could take Tate quite some time to realize she was missing—possibly days, or even a week—and by then, it could be too late.

She shook off her fear. Hope prepared herself for a very long, very painful attempt to save herself.

Chapter 13

It was going to be getting dark soon, and Jason was panicked. Okay...maybe he'd gone past panic and right to desperation. He'd hiked to Tate's house, where he'd found out that Hope had been there and left.

Hope knows the whole story.

Colter had already informed him that he'd told Hope the truth because she'd already found the receipt for the rings, and had guessed most of the plot anyway. Tate had even chewed Jason's ass for not telling her sooner, which he supposed he deserved, but not coming from Colter. He'd rather get raked over the coals by Hope. Honestly, he just wanted to *see* Hope, even if she did give him hell.

Grady had called to let Jason know none of his brothers had heard a word from Hope.

He'd left Colter's place and sprinted back to the guesthouse, only to find it still empty. He'd called Tate, and they'd started a search party. There was really no possibility that Hope could be anywhere except out here in the wilderness. There wasn't really another direct route back to the guesthouse from Colter's place, so she must have veered off the main path.

Currently, the search party had been looking for her for hours, and nobody had seen any sign of her. Tate had taken to the air in his helicopter, but there were areas he couldn't see from above, areas with thick woods that had to be searched on foot. All of Tate's brothers and Chloe were looking, and Jason knew from the map he'd gotten from Tate that he must be near the end of his assigned area. Once he hit the edge of the canyon, he'd hike down to the one opening in the canyon and head back.

He bellowed Hope's name as he swiped aside the tree branches. His heart stopped while he waited for an answer. All he'd heard so far was...silence.

Colter had sworn that Hope had seemed okay by the time she'd left his house, saying she needed a walk alone to think. Jason hoped that she wasn't thinking about how she could get out of their marriage.

I'm sorry, baby. So sorry. Answer me.

His emotions swung from fear, to remorse, to annoyance that she'd left the main path and put herself in danger. Something was wrong; he could sense it. It was almost as if his emotions were tied to Hope's, and his gut told him she wasn't just sitting somewhere, thinking about their relationship. She knew better than to be off the beaten path after dark. She hadn't taken any equipment: no flashlight, not even her cell phone. He'd found it sitting on the kitchen cupboard, plugged in and charged.

Dammit!

Tate said she didn't even have water, and it had been an unusually hot Colorado afternoon. He wiped the perspiration from his face with his already grubby t-shirt. If she was hurt or trapped somewhere, she probably couldn't even get to a water source.

His voice was hoarse as he continued to call for her and watched the sun fade behind the mountains. Pushing through more branches, he finally came to a clearing, and he could see the other wall of the canyon across from him. Moving to the edge, he studied the almost vertical drop to the bottom. It was a long, wide canyon, and she couldn't have gone any farther than here. There was only one entrance, so Tate had said his best route was to take the long hike down the incline, find the entrance and start back. The rest of the surrounding areas were an unlikely place for her to go as it was rough terrain.

"Shit!" he uttered fiercely, frustrated and desperate. He needed to find her.

"Hope!" he roared, tormented. His own voice echoed back at him from the opposite wall of the canyon, which was higher than the side he stood on.

"Here." A weak response sounded from the bottom of the canyon, and he froze. His heart palpitated wildly as he saw Hope lying in the middle of the canyon, prostrate on her back.

"Fuck!" He yanked his phone from his pocket and quickly called Tate to let him know that Hope was in the canyon, obviously hurt, but he wasn't sure how badly.

Had she fallen? That thought made Jason distraught, but he tried to calm himself down. A fall from the ledge would have killed her. With most of the floor of the canyon being rocky, she would have never survived if she had fallen.

"Hope. Hang on. I'm coming down."

"I'm okay," she called back, her voice weak. "It's just my leg."

"Just my leg," he repeated, annoyed. "Hope could probably be bleeding to death and she wouldn't admit it."

The thought of her being injured had him immediately on his ass, swinging himself around and clambering down the canyon wall. The rock had crevices, making it less difficult to climb, but going down was a challenge. It was harder to see his hand and foot holds. However, he was getting to Hope *now*. There was no way he was going all the way around and down to find the opening.

He heard her scream his name in horror as he descended as fast as he possibly could.

Hope screamed Jason's name, trying to stop him from climbing down the rock wall. It was too high, too dangerous, and he didn't even have a safety rope. It was mad for anyone to attempt a free climb down this rock face. Yet Jason was doing it, and accomplishing the task quickly.

Now she didn't dare make a sound as she watched, horrified, as he steadily made his way down the cliff. One distraction could get him killed.

Oh, God. Please let him get down safe. And then I can kill him.

Hope watched breathlessly as Jason reached the halfway point and just kept going. His powerful body took on the rock wall with determination and strength.

He's doing this for me, risking his life for me. For nothing. He could have hiked around. I could have waited.

Cursing herself quietly for crawling back to the canyon, her eyes never left Jason. She'd made it outside the canyon and into the woods. Then, she'd heard a helicopter, flying low, and she had been fairly certain a search had begun for her. Unfortunately, she'd been on her hands and knees, moving slowly. The copter had been gone before she could get clear from the cover of the trees. Sadly, she wore a green t-shirt that didn't help her stand out for anyone searching overhead. Rather than try to move on, she'd used any energy she had left to get back to the canyon and placed herself in the middle to wait for the helicopter to fly over again. She'd be visible; she'd be rescued the next time the aircraft made a pass over the canyon. It had been hot, and she was desperately thirsty, but it had been her only real choice. She didn't have the strength to make it back to the main path. Returning to the canyon, knowing they were looking for her from the air, had been the logical choice.

Hope's breath hitched as Jason's foot skidded before it found a hold as he rapidly came down the remaining part of the vertical slope. Finally, his boots hit the floor of the canyon, and Hope released her breath in a *whoosh*. She panted and trembled in the aftermath of watching him only one faulty step away from death.

He sprinted toward her and dropped to his knees by her side. "What happened? Where do you hurt? Jesus! Tell me you're really okay," he rumbled frantically, his face tormented.

Was everything that happened between you two a deception?

Tate's words haunted her. Risking his life for her was no deception on Jason's part. His expression was anguished, and that was no lie. He was terrified for her, put her well-being before his own. "I just hurt my ankle. I can't walk." She punched him in the shoulder. "Dammit! Don't ever do something like that to me again. You just took at least twenty years off my life. You could have killed yourself."

"I'm always going to take the fastest route to you." He lifted her leg onto his lap as he sat in the dirt and grass. "Fuck. This ankle is the size of a melon. What the hell did you do?"

Hope bit her lip as he gently flexed her foot. "I wasn't watching where I was going. I fell."

"Can you move it on your own?" he asked sharply.

"Barely. I can't bear weight on it." She wriggled her toes and slowly rotated her ankle with a gasp of pain.

"Stop. You need x-rays. Tate's on his way." He gave her look of both relief and anxiety, and pushed her bedraggled hair from her face. "I should have brought water, but I wanted to travel as quickly as possible."

"I'll live." Hope watched his volatile expression. She could wait until Tate arrived. "Please don't ever risk your life that way again. Promise me," she begged, her voice tremulous.

"I can't promise you that, sweetheart. I take my promises seriously, and I'd do it over and over again if I needed to get to you," he said huskily.

"You're crazy," she told him, bemused by his stubbornness. Tears trickled down her cheeks as she looked at Jason Sutherland, as bedraggled as she'd ever seen him. He looked as if he'd been drug through the dirt, and then hung out in the hot sun for hours.

"You made me that way," he answered hoarsely. "I used to be perfectly sane," he added mildly.

Hope heard the sound of an approaching helicopter, and they both went silent as they watched the aircraft land expertly, not far away from the spot where they sat.

Jason picked her up and jogged toward the helicopter, waited until the blades stopped spinning and the pilot waved them in to open the door behind the pilot seat. He placed her up on the seat and pulled himself up behind her. After he closed the door, he quickly lifted her onto his lap. "Go. She needs to get to the hospital. She injured her ankle and it could be broken. It's swollen up really bad."

The pilot removed his headphones, turned around and handed Jason a jug of water. "You look like you need this."

Not surprisingly, Tate was the pilot, and he grinned at her. "Rescued you again, H.L. Sinclair. You gonna hug me now?" He fired up the helicopter.

Hope gave him a weak smile. "Maybe next time," she answered sassily.

"You'll touch her over my dead body," Jason answered irritably.

"That can be arranged," Tate shot back with a brash smile.

"Hospital, Colter. Let's move," Jason growled. He handed Hope the water first and helped her tip it up. When she'd had her fill, Jason chugged part of the bottle before he put it on the seat next to him.

"I'm going. Jeeezus! Mission accomplished, Sutherland. Chill out," Tate answered calmly as he turned around and put his headphones back on.

Tate had the bird in motion quickly, rising up so fast that Hope felt as if she'd left her stomach on the ground.

"Fuck. He flies like a bat out of hell," Jason complained loudly.

"You asked for it." Hope laid her head on his shoulder, her mouth near his ear so he could hear her over the noise of the helicopter. "I've been with him in a helicopter before."

Hope still remembered the harrowing flight to safety Tate had made after they'd rescued her. Tate didn't do anything slow. He was meticulous, fast, and probably very deadly. She'd never seen him that way, but she didn't doubt that he could be lethal underneath that cocky smile and teasing demeanor.

"During your rescue?" Jason asked coarsely, his body tense.

"Yeah. He always seems to push everything to the limit. He flew the same way when he was in Special Forces. He's good."

"He's an asshole sometimes," Jason retorted tightly.

"He saved my life. I think he saved a lot of lives. I can give him a pass on being arrogant just because of that," Hope said soberly.

"What was that shit about hugging him?" Jason asked heatedly.

Hope shrugged. "I hugged him because I was so happy to see him and I was grateful to him. He thinks he's irresistible." She had to admit, Tate was breathtakingly gorgeous, and that small dimple did make him totally fascinating and alluring. Understandably, his aura of danger and mystery added to his personality would make him an unholy temptation to most women. But Hope wasn't most women, and the only chemistry she felt was with the man who held her lovingly, protectively, the guy who had literally scaled a mountain to help her.

Jason.

"No more hugging men unless it's me," Jason demanded.

Hope smiled against his shoulder. "I do have brothers."

"Fine. Just them."

"He did pick us up, and he is taking us to the hospital at warp speed," Hope said teasingly. "Maybe I could just give him a small peck on the cheek later?" She poked at the tiger, and she knew it, but she couldn't help herself. The more possessive Jason became, the more secure she felt. Right now, she needed that reassurance. She was sick from the heat and hurting. It took her mind off her bodily pain.

"You want to kiss him?" Jason sounded appalled and disgruntled.

"Please. Just to say thank you," she spurred him on.

"No. I don't want your lips or body anywhere near Colter in the future," he argued fiercely. His arms tightened around her waist greedily. "All he'd have to do is smell your intoxicating scent and he'd try to steal you away."

Smirking against his shoulder because he seemed to be under the impression that she was irresistible to any man, she answered, "Right now, I stink."

"You're still not kissing him," he answered adamantly.

"We'll see," she answered mysteriously. The helicopter descended for a landing.

He grunted, annoyed, but he answered, "At the moment, all I care about is you. It looks like we're at the hospital. Are you still hurting?"

She nodded hesitantly. Her ankle throbbed agonizingly, but she didn't want Jason to know how badly she hurt. "I'll be fine."

"I'm so sorry, Hope. You'll never know how much," he replied huskily, his voice emanating regret and remorse.

She opened her mouth to reply, to try to alleviate some of his self-castigation, but the door to the helicopter flew open. Helping hands assisted her to a gurney that had been brought out to the helicopter pad.

Once situated, several bodies pushed the gurney toward the entrance to the ER. One older man asked rapid-fire questions and forced her to turn her attention away from Jason to answer him.

They sent her to x-ray almost immediately. Jason waited in the room for her with a discontented, worried expression.

Hope smiled at him as they wheeled her away, to reassure him she'd be fine. Maybe she *would* make him grovel, but there was no doubt in her mind that Jason Sutherland loved her. His heart-stopping scramble down the sheer mountain cliff had been more than enough to convince her, and she'd thought about everything that had happened between the two of them since they'd arrived here in Rocky Springs. Yes, he'd been wrong. Yes, he'd sometimes been an asshole. But his concern had always been there, and his tenderness wrenched her heart.

She was in the ER for hours, but once she'd returned from x-ray, Jason had been waiting for her, and he never left her side again.

Chapter 14

The next day, Hope got a phone call from each one of her brothers, all of them angry as hell at Jason. By the time she got to Grady's call, the last brother to contact her, she was done hearing all of them beat up Jason verbally.

She was back in her bed at the guesthouse, her ankle elevated. It wasn't broken, but it was badly sprained. The swelling was already down from ice and anti-inflammatory medication, and the pain was almost nonexistent unless she tried to bear weight on her right foot. She'd be up and around shortly. The ankle just needed some time to heal.

Jason had waited on her hand and foot, stayed with her constantly, and fetched anything she wanted or needed. He stood at the foot of the bed and frowned as she talked to Grady on the phone.

"I swear I'm going to put his balls into his throat when I see him. Emily's packing right now. We're on our way," Grady told her gruffly.

Hope sighed. She'd already explained to every one of her brothers that Jason was taking very good care of her, and she didn't want for anything. She'd be fine as soon as she was up and around.

Grady proved to be the most stubborn, probably because he was closest to Jason, and felt betrayed. "You're not going to touch his balls," Hope told Grady calmly. "I like them exactly where they are."

"He lied to you," Grady said furiously. "He manipulated you."

"I lied to him, too, Grady." Her eyes met Jason's as she held her cell phone to her ear, her back against the headboard. They hadn't had a chance to discuss anything yet, Jason making his priority just taking care of her. "I'm not happy about how everything happened." Jason's expression turned to one of regret. "But the problem is…I love him. I love him so much that I want this marriage to last forever, no matter how it happened."

Jason's head jerked up higher; his eyes narrowed on her face.

"Yeah, he said he loved you, too. But I don't like the way he went about getting you to marry him," Grady's voice grumbled through the phone line.

"He said that?" Hope's heart thundered as she looked at Jason and he nodded his head, his eyes bright and intense.

"He did," Grady affirmed. "I'm worried, Hope. I just want you to be happy."

"I am happy." A tear trickled down her cheek. All of her brothers had expressed their concern, and it was genuine. She might not have been able to be really close to them, but she wanted that to change. "I love you, Grady. I'm so glad you have Emily. I'm going to be as happy with Jason as you are with Em," she told him reassuringly.

"You're my baby sister. It's my job to worry," Grady replied, his voice graveled and emotional. "And I love you, too, Hope. I don't want you to be married to the wrong guy."

"I'm not. I married the perfect man for me. I know you're upset with Jason, but you know him. You know what kind of person he is. He risked his life by descending a rock wall that no climber should be climbing down without safety equipment just to get to me. And all I had was a sprained ankle. Do you really think he'd hurt me intentionally? I like to think that he lied because he was so out of his mind with lust that he would do anything to have me," she told her brother teasingly.

Jason nodded again, emphatically this time, his eyes fixated on hers.

"Please. I don't want to hear about one of my best friend's and my baby sister's sex life, although I do know exactly what he was feeling," Grady said hastily. "Just tell me one more time, honestly, that you're okay."

"I'm more than okay," she told him softly. "I'm in love with Jason."

Jason gaped at her, as though he were awed to hear her say it again.

"Tell him he's lucky we don't all kick his ass," Grady grunted.

"I wouldn't let you lay a hand on him. I like his handsome face and hot backside exactly the way it is—thank you very much," she flipped back at Grady.

"Spare me the details," Grady begged.

Hope laughed, a delighted chuckle because her brother seemed to be completely grossed out by hearing anything sexual about her and Jason. "Give my love to Emily," Hope requested.

"I can definitely do that," her brother answered. "Call me tomorrow. I want to hear from you every day or I'll come there to make sure you're okay."

"I'll call." She disconnected the phone after they had said their goodbyes.

Jason came forward slowly, took the phone from her hand and sank to his knees beside the bed. "Did you mean it?" he asked hesitantly, vulnerably.

"Yes." She looked him straight in the eyes. The tears continued to flow down her face. "Did you?"

"I love you more than I love anything or anyone else in this world, Hope." He grasped her hand and entwined their fingers together. "I'd take back how our marriage happened in a heartbeat if I could, but I can't make myself regret being married to you. I want it too much. I love you too much." His voice cracked with emotion as he squeezed her fingers. "Can you forgive me?"

Remembering that she was going to make him grovel, she asked, "How badly do you want my forgiveness?" She'd already forgiven him the moment he'd risked his life for her, maybe even before that, but she wasn't quite ready to tell him that yet.

"I want it bad enough to spend the rest of my life making it up to you. You'll always come first in my life, sweetheart. And I'll never lie to you again."

"Why did you do it?"

Jason grimaced. "For the exact reason that you told Grady you were hoping for on the phone. I was out of my mind for you, and when I heard that you were getting married, I couldn't let you marry anyone else but me."

"Were you ever going to tell me?" she asked curiously, not wanting to think that he'd never planned to tell her the truth.

"Yes. I couldn't live with myself or you if I didn't. I was planning on telling you as soon as I got back from town. Hence, the flowers." Jason nodded at the large bouquet that now sat on the dresser for her to enjoy. "And a few other things I picked up."

"You were trying to bribe me to forgive you?" Her lips twitched to keep from smiling. Jason looked so forlorn that she didn't want him to think she was laughing at him.

"No. I wanted to make you happy," he said earnestly.

Hope swiped at her tears. Honestly, Jason's sadness killed her. "The flowers are beautiful. Thank you."

Jason looked at her hopefully. "I got a couple of other little things, too." He got up and hastened to the closet, coming back with a large bag. He pulled out a small box first. "I hope you like this."

Hope took it from him; it was from the same store where he'd bought their rings. As she popped the lid, the necklace on the red velvet of the box left her stunned. It wasn't ostentatious, but it was gorgeous, the heart a lovely symbol of love. "It's incredible," she told him breathlessly. He hadn't bought her the biggest or the showiest of jewels, although she knew it was costly. Jason had given her his heart symbolically, and it was beautiful.

He helped her put it on, and he got a mirror so she could see how it looked. "I wanted you to be able to wear this every day, carry my heart with you all the time. The emerald reminds me of the color of your eyes. I'll get something bigger later," he told her hesitantly.

"Don't you dare." She grabbed his hand urgently. "I love this. I'll never take it off. I don't want anything else."

"We'll see," Jason shot back noncommittally, giving her own words back to her with a mischievous smile. He handed her the bag. "I hope this will work for you."

Hope peeked into the bag and gasped when she pulled out his gift. It was a top-of-the-line camera that could be used underwater. "It's wonderful. But I don't shoot underwater."

"I'm hoping you will someday—or at least from my boat. I think you'd like snorkeling. With your eye for color, you'd love shooting underwater in the Bahamas."

Hope smiled and crossed her arms. "You keep calling it a boat. Exactly how big is your little boat?"

"It's not all that small. It's around seventy feet, with incredibly comfortable cabins," Jason admitted sheepishly. "But it's not gigantic."

Hope let out a startled laugh. "It *is* gigantic."

"She's named after you," Jason confessed. "It wasn't a coincidence. And I couldn't buy just any old boat if I was naming her after you."

Jason would never buy any old boat. He was a billionaire, and he liked the finer things. The fact that he didn't consider his "boat" a yacht amused her, and she was touched and surprised that he'd named *Sutherland's Hope* after her. "She's really named for me?" she asked tentatively. "Why?"

Jason moved to the other side of the bed, scooted close to her carefully, and eased himself onto the bed to keep from jostling her ankle. Sliding his arm around her shoulders, he rested his back on the headboard and pulled her head onto his shoulder. "I think I've probably been in love with you since you were eighteen," he started out thoughtfully as he stroked a hand over her hair. "I've had a hard-on for you ever since. Every time I saw you after your high school graduation was difficult for me, and I guess over the holidays, I lost it. Finally, there was no boyfriend, you were finally available, and I was elated. Even if you were Grady's sister, I couldn't ignore how attracted I was to you anymore. I was devastated when I got up and you were gone after our night together. It destroyed me when I heard you were actually marrying the boyfriend you'd broken up with months before."

Jason released a long, masculine sigh. "What you said to Grady is true. I did want you so desperately that I wasn't willing to let you marry anyone else." His body tensed. "I didn't think about the consequences, Hope. All I could think about was somebody else touching you, holding what belonged to me. When Tate made his crazy plan, I agreed readily. I was willing to do anything, even face your wrath, to have you. I was worried that you'd be miserable with a loser, but most of my motivations were strictly selfish. I wanted you for myself."

Hope was floored. She had never realized that Jason felt the same things she had all these years. "Do you remember the wedding?"

"Of course. I picked the rings. I planned on getting you wasted so I could marry you. I'm not going to lie about it anymore," he said fiercely. "I told myself I'd let you go once we'd satisfied ourselves, but that was never going to happen. It just took me awhile to admit it to myself. I was angry with you for marrying someone else after what happened on New Year's."

"But he wasn't real."

"I didn't know that," he countered.

"How was the wedding?"

"For me, it was the happiest day of my life, even if you were intoxicated. I put my ring on your finger and you became mine after years of torture. Purely selfish...but true. We got married by a justice of the peace, and it was short. Tate stood up for me, and I found a young woman to stand as witness for you. I'm sorry. It wasn't the wedding you deserved, and we can get married again—the right way this time." Jason rubbed her back and shoulders comfortingly.

"I don't think the wedding is important. It's the marriage you have after the wedding that matters," she told him thoughtfully. Honestly, she didn't care how it happened, as long as it was legal. She belonged to Jason, and it was how they went on from here that mattered. "The thing is, I've always felt the same way about you. I have since I saw you at my graduation. That was why I was still a virgin when I was attacked. Nobody ever measured up to you."

"I should have told you a long time ago how I felt, how much I wanted you," Jason rasped, sounding disgusted with himself.

"We can't change the past, Jason. Can we just go on from here?" Hope didn't want to think about the past now that they were together. They couldn't change things, go back and redo anything. But they could have the happiest life imaginable together. "I love you." She let out a happy sigh. "And I've always been waiting for you."

"I waited for you, too, Peaches." He dropped a sweet kiss on her forehead. "I'm sorry that I lied. Are you going to let me out of the doghouse?"

"I don't think I have a choice." She tried to make her voice sound beleaguered. "I love you now. And you've ruined me. I'm addicted to you."

"Sweetheart, I've been ruined since you turned eighteen. I love you. Forgive me. Please," he begged gravely. "It will kill me if you don't."

"Okay," she said dreamily, agreeably. A remorseful Jason was hard to resist, and he'd groveled long enough. Hope just wanted to get on with loving him, and having him loving her back. "I'm so easy."

"You're anything but easy. It's taken me years to make you mine," Jason said dubiously. "And now you're going to scare the shit out of me every day with your career. I have to admit I have a love/hate relationship with your fearlessness."

"I'm not fearless," she whispered huskily. "And I'm not going to chase storms anymore." She'd made her decision after she'd talked to Tate. "When I first started doing it, I was excited. I loved the adrenaline rush, and I wanted to make a name for myself. After I was…kidnapped, I had to go back to prove something to myself. You were right when you said I didn't need to prove anything to a dead man anymore. I actually don't think the last few years have been about conquering my fears. I'd already done that. I think I was disconnected and lonely, and I didn't know anything else. Lying to my family had separated me from my brothers, and I kept everyone else at a distance because I was used to it. I don't want to do that anymore," she finished breathlessly.

"Thank Christ," Jason blurted out emphatically. "I don't want you to quit if you really love it, but if you don't want to do it anymore, I'd be fucking ecstatic."

Hope laughed. "Then be ecstatic because I think I'd like to take some underwater pictures, and I really love doing my landscape and wilderness shots. I still love storms, but I think I was chasing them for the wrong reasons. I was lonely, and I didn't know how to be any other way."

"Not anymore, sweetheart. You have me, and you can let yourself be close to your brothers again now that you don't have to cover anything up."

"I'd like that," she answered happily. "Do you think I should tell them everything?"

"Your call, baby. I'll stand behind whatever you want to do. But I don't think you need to do it because of them. I think you only need to do that if *you* want it."

"Maybe someday I will tell them. Right now, I'd just like to spend some time being happy with my husband, and see what it feels like to not be lonely anymore."

Jason fiddled with a lock of her hair. "Me, too. I've been restless and moody for a long time because I missed you."

"Filling your time working for charities?" she asked curiously.

"Actually, yeah. I have my own work to do, but I think I've found more satisfaction from starting this organization for battered women than anything else I've ever done." He hesitated for a moment. "Tate must have told you."

"He did. I think you're amazing, Jason Sutherland. Can I donate? I have a very rich husband now, so I don't need to worry about money," she teased him mercilessly.

"Keep your money safe," he advised. "I've donated enough for both of us. Put it in safe investments and leave it for our children."

Hope's heart accelerated. "Are we having kids?"

"I sure as hell hope so," Jason answered emphatically. "I'd love to have a sweet little girl just like her mother."

Hope's heart stuttered. "I didn't think I'd ever have children, but I'd like to someday." She'd always loved kids, but had never imagined herself being that intimate with a man. "Do you know a good investment counselor who can help my money grow for my children?"

"I know the very best," he said arrogantly.

Hope laughed merrily and stroked his whiskered cheek lovingly. "I'm sure you do," she whispered, leaning over to kiss him tenderly on the lips. Her heart swelled as he kissed her with a gentle affection that made her feel wanted...and very much loved. "Does he have a boat so I can take underwater photos? He might just be the man of my dreams," she told him as she pulled back and left her lips only inches from his.

"Baby, I don't know if you were dreaming about me, but I've had more wet dreams about you than I can count, and I *am* your man. I always will be," he told her bossily.

Hope could feel his hot breath caress her mouth, and she froze for a moment, loving the warm intimacy of his possessiveness. "I think you're right. You're perfect." She smiled as she breached the distance between their lips and gave him an embrace that wouldn't leave him with any doubt where her heart was, and how much she loved him.

He let out a strangled groan as his tongue entwined gently with hers, a triumphant, ardent sound from a man who had just gotten everything he wanted...and more.

Chapter 15

A week later, Hope limped into the bedroom of the guesthouse, curious to see where all of the noise she could hear from the living room came from. She'd been working on her photos on her computer, but the incessant pounding sounds coming from the bedroom had intrigued her.

Her ankle was better, although Jason spent most of his time carrying her around. At this rate, he'd be babying her for the rest of her life. It wasn't that she didn't enjoy being treasured, but she missed him, and she wanted to drop her panties every time she looked at him. Unfortunately, he was having none of that, afraid he'd hurt her ankle if he did anything other than give her a gentle kiss, and he held her as if she were as fragile as blown glass.

God, she loved him. Jason took care of her completely, but she needed him to touch her, and she needed him to fuck her or she was going to die of frustration.

They were headed back to New York tomorrow; Jason needed to take care of some business there. He'd been worried about her being unhappy in the city, but she'd assured him that as long as they were together, she'd be blissfully content. He had a job to do, responsibilities, and she was perfectly fine with living in his pent-house for a while. He'd decided he didn't want to live there full-time, and that was fine with her. She'd follow him just about anywhere. They still had her condo in Aspen to escape to, and she had her lovely house in Amesport, Maine. His idea was to eventually travel to New York for business only and make their home in Amesport.

Hope had been ecstatic, thrilled that she'd be close to Grady again. She really liked Emily, and she knew she'd make new friends in Amesport through Grady and Emily. She was more than willing to live there for most of the year, after Jason wrapped some things up in New York. Something told her that Jason would like to be closer to his mother and Grady, too.

Her feet hit the plush carpet in the bedroom, and she peeked into the bathroom. Jason stood in front of the bathroom mirror.

He'd been putting it back on the wall.

"Disposing of the kinky evidence?" she asked him merrily.

"Why are you out of your chair?" He turned and gave her a stern look.

"Because I need to walk occasionally, and it doesn't hurt to put weight on my ankle anymore." She examined the mirror and then went to the bed to look under the canopy. "It looks good. I'd never be able to tell." She giggled.

"I told you I was good with tools." He moved behind her to wrap his arms around her waist.

Turning, she put her arms around his neck. "You're a man with many talents. You're good at a lot of things." *You're great at making me orgasm. Please do it.*

Taking the initiative, her patience gone, Hope opened his but-toned-down shirt.

"Hope. It's too soon." He groaned and caught her roaming hands in his. "I don't want to hurt you."

"I already hurt." She moved one of his hands down between her thighs. "I ache, and nobody can fix that except you. Fuck me, Jason. I can't wait any longer."

"Fuck," he growled. "It's hard for me, too, Hope."

She reached down and fondled his erection over his jeans. "I can see that it is," she murmured seductively. "I can fix that." She pulled her other hand from his and finished unbuttoning his shirt. "Please. I'm fine. I need you."

Jason speared his hands into her hair. "I don't want to fuck you, even though I love it when you talk dirty to me. I want to make love to you, baby."

"I want that, too," she confided. With his shirt now open, she placed wet kisses on his chest. "I want to touch you."

Jason tore the shirt down his arms and groaned. "Touch me, then. Just let me know if I hurt you."

Her core flooded as she ran her palms down his muscular chest, over his powerful biceps and down his back. He felt like hot, hard sin, and she already trembled with the need to have him inside her.

Her hands went to his jeans, fumbled with the buttons until they were all open. Jason pulled them down, taking his boxer briefs with them, and stepped out of them before he reached for the bottom of Hope's summer shirt. She lifted her arms obediently, ready to be naked, feel them skin-to-skin. "It seems like it's been forever," she told him plaintively.

"I know," he answered roughly. "And it's only been a week."

Hope pulled the drawstring on her shorts, wriggled them down with her panties and let Jason pull them off her feet gently.

He laid her lightly on the bed. "I took the mirror down," he reminded her, as he came between her open thighs.

She wrapped her arms around his neck. "I don't need it. You know that. Make love to me the way you want to, Jason. I need to feel you inside me."

She shuddered as his body came over hers, relieved as their bare skin finally connected. Her nipples were hard, and his chest abraded the sensitized peaks.

Hope let out an elated sigh; the feel and scent of Jason drove her desire. Thrusting her hands into his hair, she gasped. "I love you."

Jason fisted his hands in her hair; his mouth roamed over every inch of the delicate skin on her neck and lingered to flick out his tongue and taste her flesh. "I love you," he answered back, his voice muffled against her throat.

He took his time, his lips moving over her shoulders and down to her breasts. He took one of the hard nipples between his lips, worshipped it with his mouth before he paid homage to the other one. Hope whimpered as she held his head to her breasts, needing more, needing him.

"Jason. Please." Hope wasn't going to be able to endure his teasing for very long.

Moving up her body carefully, his tempestuous, covetous gaze roamed over her face before he lowered his mouth to hers.

Hope stroked her fingers over his neck and down his back; she met his kiss with the same urgency as his. Their tongues entwined and meshed, fusing them together. She moaned with the ecstasy of being in this intimate position, the two of them melding together. Her legs wrapped around his hips, she bucked against him, eager to feel him conjoined with her.

Tearing his mouth from hers, his chest heaving, he told her gently, "Easy, baby." He pinned her hands over her head and held them tightly. Jason looked at her possessively, his blue eyes swirling and turbulent. "Mine. You belong to me." Although his tone was covetous, it was also awed, incredulous.

"Forever," she whispered, feeling his need along with her own. "Make love to me, Jason." She loved his bossy possession in the bedroom, and it ramped up her need, heated her body until she felt as if she was going to go up in flames.

He reached one of his hands down between them, held her wrists in one hand, and ran his fingers through her drenched, torrid folds. He hissed as he found her clit. "You're so responsive, so wet for me."

"Only for you," she keened, wanting him inside her.

"I love the way your body responds to me," he whispered huskily near her temple. His warm breath wafted tantalizingly over her ear.

Hope cried out as he teased her clit. His thumb first circled the pulsating mass of nerves and then rolled over it with not quite enough pressure. He released her wrists to grasp her ass.

She raked her fingernails down his back, pushed her heels into his ass to make him act.

"Mark me," he grunted. "God, I fucking love that. Make me yours, Hope. I've always been yours."

His words inflamed her, and she cried out his name as he thrust powerfully into her sheath and buried himself to the root of his cock. "Yes," she mewled as she dug her nails into his back. "Oh, Jason, you feel so good."

"You feel incredible, sweetheart." He groaned. His cock moved out and then back in with a powerful stroke, both hands now on her ass to keep her positioned right where he wanted her. He pulled her up to meet every entry; their skin slapped together with the force of their joining.

Hope moaned, touched every inch of Jason her fingers could find, moved over his back and down to his ass, grasped his tight rear end and urged him to take her harder, faster.

Jason shifted and pummeled in and out of her channel, stimulating her clit.

"Yes. Please," she begged. Her body shuddered, heat shooting through her belly and down to her core.

"I love you, baby. Come for me," he demanded. His thrusts went deeper, faster. He leaned forward and captured her mouth; his tongue speared between her lips and mimicked the hard, fast strokes he gave her with his cock.

I love you. I love you. I love you.

The words pounded through her mind as her body came apart, and she held onto Jason as she spun out of control and her core clenched around him. She moaned into his mouth, and felt his responding groan.

She climaxed just like that, her mouth fused to Jason's. His cock pounded into her as she pulsated around him and made him find his own release.

Tearing his mouth from hers, he let his body rest on top of her, as though he didn't want to separate them. Hope could feel his heart hammer against her breasts, and they both tried to catch their breath as they lay there stunned and sated.

"Shit. I'm too heavy for you," Jason said, disgruntled. He rolled to her side and pulled her gently on top of him. "Is your ankle okay?"

Hope couldn't even feel her ankle. Her body was so sated, her mind so at peace that she'd never feel a tiny pain in her leg. "It's fine." She panted and stroked her palm over the rough stubble on his cheek.

She felt overwhelmed, her emotions running high. Tears poured down her face as she choked out, "I love you so much."

"Sweetheart, what's wrong?" Jason was immediately sobered. He placed his hands on both sides of her head so he could look at her.

"I'm happy," she sobbed. "I'm so damn happy. I never knew it could be like this." She'd only ever known sex as a violent act until Jason. "You're amazing."

He swiped at her tears gently and placed her head on his chest. "It should always be like this. I hate what you went through, Hope," he told her roughly, intensely, his voice full of pain.

Lifting her head, she looked at him tenderly. "Don't. Don't think about the past. Think about how happy we are now. I'm glad I survived or I'd never have this. I wouldn't have you."

"I wish you had me and you'd never had to go through that," he answered in a graveled, emotional tone.

Hope knew it was going to take awhile for Jason to not think about the incident every single day, but hopefully he'd eventually think about it less and less. "It's in the past now. Thanks to you, I'm a different woman than I was a few weeks ago."

"You've always been the same woman, Hope. And you've always been mine." His arms tightened around her, and she felt his big body shudder.

Eventually, Hope was optimistic that Jason would get over what had happened to her. Every day, it got better, the experience leaving her mind almost completely as it was replaced with memories of Jason. As time went by, she'd remind him every day how happy he made her, how much she loved him, and that horrible experience would fade away. It would have to. No one could experience this much joy without it eventually pushing away bad memories.

"You're right. I've always been yours." Her heart swelled with love as she ran the back of her hand down his cheek and then buried her hand in his coarse, beautiful *fuck-me* hair.

Truthfully, Jason had had her heart for as long as she could remember, first as her boy hero, and then as a man. She'd never been a big believer in destiny or fate, but it felt to her as if she was meant to belong with Jason since she was a child. She'd just needed to grow up.

"I'm glad I'm all grown up now," she said with a happy sigh.

"Thank Christ," Jason echoed. "I was getting tired of waiting."

"You could have married another woman," she teased.

"There is no other woman for me," he growled, but he tangled his fingers in her hair gently.

They didn't move for a very long time. They lay there just celebrating the joy of being together, and looking forward to their future. They murmured about their love, and healed old wounds that had kept them apart.

When they finally left Rocky Springs the next day, Hope *did* kiss Tate on the cheek and thanked him for everything he'd done for her. He might be cocksure and arrogant sometimes, but the man had a heart of gold lying beneath his alpha exterior.

"I hope Tate finds a good woman someday," Hope said wistfully as they made their way to Jason's private jet to fly back to New York.

"Oh, me too, sweetheart. And I hope she puts him through hell before she puts him out of misery. Arrogant bastard," he grumbled.

Hope smiled as she walked beside Jason, her hand entwined with his as they made their way to the aircraft. "That's a terrible thing to say." She slugged him in the bicep playfully. She knew Jason actually liked Tate, probably respected him, but he hadn't been happy when she'd hugged the handsome blond man goodbye and pecked him on the cheek.

"It's not terrible. I'm actually waiting for it to happen," he said innocently, shooting her a slick glance.

"You're waiting to torture him," she chastised.

Hope smiled as Jason laughed evilly. She couldn't help herself. Being raised with four brothers who tormented each other constantly, she knew they still cared about each other, and Jason was far from coldhearted. Tate might be a pain in Jason's ass, but he liked him.

"Maybe a little," Jason admitted as he helped her up the stairs of the plane. "I was fine until you kissed him," he accused.

Hope just gave him a seductive smile. "He just got a friendly peck on the cheek. You get a hell of a lot more."

"Show me," Jason said huskily as he followed her onto the plane.

"Count on it," she replied in the *fuck-me* voice that she knew he couldn't refuse.

"Soon," Jason growled.

Hope just laughed, and proceeded to show him a lot of things as soon as the plane had leveled off and they were on their way to New York. It was a flight that passed...very pleasurably.

Epilogue

Two Weeks Later

Jason watched Hope as she sat at the bow of the yacht. Yeah, he now called *Sutherland's Hope* a yacht. His wife wasn't worthy of anything less. She looked beautiful enough and happy enough to take his breath away. He doubted he'd ever look at her and not feel the exact same way. She'd become his entire life, a life that had made him so happy that it was almost terrifying.

She'd come on board the yacht full of excitement and enthusiasm, anxious to be out on the water. Looking at her, he could tell she would become as addicted to being on the ocean as he was. She was already involved in shooting pictures of just about anything and everything she saw.

Her hair was loose and blowing wildly in the breeze, making her look untamed and sexy as hell.

"Having fun?" He took a seat beside her.

"This is incredible. Thank you for bringing me out," she answered enthusiastically.

Like he'd do anything else? He couldn't be away from her for a day without missing her so much it hurt.

They'd spent most of yesterday visiting with his mom, and she'd been ecstatic about Hope joining the family. His mother had always adored all of the Sinclairs, but she'd had a soft spot for the little girl who really had no mother to guide her, and a useless, abusive father. She'd welcomed Hope like family, and Jason had seen Hope glow from being treated like an adored daughter.

"I'm glad you like it," he told her simply as he dropped a kiss on her forehead.

"I love it. I've already gotten some beautiful shots."

Jason grinned. He hoped to turn her mind to a different view as they headed out to sea. "I haven't shown you the comfortable cabins yet."

She smirked at him. "Is that all you ever think about?"

"When I'm around you? Yep. Pretty much." Jason wasn't going to deny he wanted to get her into a bed. Any bed. All he had to do was look at her, think about her, and he was rock-hard.

What a fool he'd been to think he'd ever fuck Hope out of his system. Instead of getting easier, it was actually harder to keep his hands off her as they grew closer and closer.

He still had more business to finish up in New York, but later in the year, they hoped to move permanently to Amesport. They might hit Aspen occasionally to ski, and he'd still have to be in New York sometimes, but they'd have a permanent home, and Hope would be somewhere she enjoyed. Not once did she complain about New York. She was the type of woman who found good in everything, and she spent time exploring the sights and took as many pictures as possible. But he suspected that she'd be a hell of a lot happier in Amesport, and if he was honest, so would he. It would be nice to have Grady and Emily right down the street.

"Think Grady has cooled down enough for me to show my face in Maine by now?" he asked casually.

"He's over how we started completely. You've talked to him. He's anxious to have us to live there." She swiped her windblown hair back from her face.

Much to Jason's relief, her brothers had gotten over what he'd done. Probably because they spoke to Hope often, and they knew she was happy.

"I'm glad," he admitted. "Grady and I have been friends for a long time."

"You're still friends," she told him adamantly as she threaded her fingers through his hair and pulled his head down for a steamy kiss.

Jason groaned. He needed to show her the cabins soon. As their mouths separated, he said persuasively, "Come below."

"But it's beautiful up here," she protested mildly and threw him a wicked smile.

"Something will be beautiful down below, too."

"Won't the crew think it's odd that we've already disappeared below deck?"

"They work for me," he replied cockily.

"I guess I could use a nap. Somebody kept me up late last night," she admonished him playfully.

He picked her up, and headed toward the stairs. "Sweetheart, I think you'll still be tired."

"Then maybe we shouldn't," she pondered teasingly. Her arms wrapped around his neck.

"We should," he insisted as he took her down the stairs. She was so damn beautiful, there was no way he was letting her nap until later. Much later.

"I love you," she murmured into his ear.

Holy shit. He moved faster, letting Hope open the door as they arrived at the cabin. "I love you, baby."

"So what do you think?" he asked nervously.

"Beautiful," Hope answered reverently. "I can't believe you've never screwed a woman on this yacht. You've had it for a few years."

"I couldn't. This was my hope—or my Hope, actually. It wasn't going to happen."

"A real virgin yacht, huh?"

"Pure as the driven snow, if you don't count the times I got off to fantasies about you being with me." He'd had many of those.

"Let's make your dreams come true," she told him quietly, seriously.

"Baby, they already have."

He kissed her, and she proceeded to bring his every fantasy to life, and she succeeded, making reality far better than fantasy.

He'd waited a lifetime for Hope, and every moment with her was better than the last.

Jason had decided that sometimes, miraculous things really were worth the wait.

~The End~

Please visit me at:
http://www.authorjsscott.com
http://www.facebook.com/authorjsscott

You can write to me at
jsscott_author@hotmail.com

You can also tweet
@AuthorJSScott

Please sign up for my Newsletter for updates,
new releases and exclusive excerpts.

Books by J. S. Scott:

The Billionaire's Obsession Series:

The Billionaire's Obsession

Heart Of The Billionaire

The Billionaire's Salvation

The Billionaire's Game

Billionaire Undone

Billionaire Unmasked

The Vampire Coalition Series:

The Vampire Coalition: The Complete Collection

Ethan's Mate

Rory's Mate

Nathan's Mate

Liam's Mate

Daric's Mate

The Sentinel Demons:

A Dangerous Bargain

A Dangerous Hunger

The Curve Collection: Big Girls And Bad Boys

The Changeling Encounters Collection

34900227R00124

Made in the USA
Lexington, KY
25 August 2014